Watson is Not an Idiot

An Opinionated Tour of the Sherlock Holmes Canon

By Eddy Webb

Paperback ISBN 978-1-78092-496-0
ePub ISBN 978-1-78092-497-7
PDF ISBN 978-1-78092-498-4

Published in the UK by MX Publishing
335 Princess Park Manor, Royal Drive,
London, N11 3GX
www.mxpublishing.co.uk

Cover design by www.staunch.com

To my grandfather, who instilled in me a passion for mysteries.

To my mother, who instilled in me a habit of reading.

And to my wife, who instilled in me the courage to write.

I could not have made this book what it is without the incredible help of my editor, Genevieve Podleski, and my beta readers: Maria Cambone, Laura Desnoit, and Kara Swenson. Also, my sincerest thanks to Steve Emecz for being a wonderful publisher.

Contents

7

Introduction

I've been a Sherlock Holmes fan for most of my life. One of my first "grown-up" books was a worn compilation of *Adventures* and *Memoirs* given to me by my grandfather, and I devoured it. I didn't understand all the words (and the ones I did understand caused me to regularly fail spelling tests because I confused American and British spellings through my childhood), but I loved every page. I didn't quite understand why it was important to study the fact that bruises wouldn't form on a corpse, or why there were a wide variety of tobaccos that left an equally wide variety of ash. All I knew is that when Holmes admonished Watson for not knowing how many stairs there were leading up to their rooms at 221B Baker Street in "A Scandal in Bohemia," I went right home and made sure to count the number of stairs leading up to my bedroom (thirteen), so that I would be ready whenever that information became important in a murder investigation.

Much like Dr. Watson, my time with the Great Detective has gone through cycles. Sometimes I spent weeks or months in close company with him, while other times it was years between visits. But he was never far from my mind, and recently I've been thinking of him more than ever. Some years ago, the incomparable Ken Hite released a series of essays, critiques, and rants on his LiveJournal about each of the H. P. Lovecraft stories, which he entitled *Tour de Lovecraft* (later compiled into a book by Atomic Overmind Press, which is definitely worth checking out if you're into Lovecraft). I mentioned to him in passing at the time that I should probably get around to doing a similar series based on the original Holmes canon. I remember his response being encouraging, but for some reason I don't recall it clearly —

perhaps I have blocked the incident from my mind for my own sanity. But since the release of the Guy Ritchie films, the BBC series *Sherlock*, and the CBS series *Elementary*, Holmes has had a new revival in popular culture, and I spend more and more time talking with people about the Great Detective, as well as (more often than not) getting into Internet arguments about him.

Sherlock Holmes is one of the most widely-recognized literary characters in the world, and yet many fans haven't actually read the original stories. Most people's perceptions come from vague recollections of Basil Rathbone and Nigel Bruce, or from when they were forced to read *Hound of the Baskervilles* in school. The popular culture understanding of Holmes and his world is now a mythology: full of wonderful stories that bear only a passing resemblance to the facts. There are very few people who grew up on Holmes like I did, reading the canon first before experiencing the larger world of Sherlock Holmes afterwards. Those who approach Holmes from the other direction need a guide, someone who can take the hand of the reader either diving into the canon for the first time (you lucky bastard) or who hasn't read it in years. These new readers need a guide who can answer questions or point out dangerous bits along the way. More often than not, my friends turned to me to be that guide.

Thus, this book. Originally a collection of over seventy essays published on my blog, *Watson is Not an Idiot* chronicles my rereading of the entire canon. Like Dr. Watson, I am not a reliable narrator, nor am I an objective critic — my relationship with Holmes is too entrenched and complex for me to be able to act as either. Instead, I point out interesting things and mention personal gripes. Sometimes, I check my facts with essays and books by far more educated people. Other times, I go off on unhinged rants about certain aspects of the stories. For this book, I've rewritten many of the essays to expand on some points, correct whatever errors I could find, and provide even more of my opinionated slant on the canon.

How you use this book is up to you, although you will need your own copy of the original stories. I do encourage you to read the stories in the publication order of the books where you can (I used the American publication of the stories for this book — a fact that will become important as you make your way through). The actual chronology of the cases is a hopeless mess that is still being debated over a hundred years later, so that is a lost cause. Besides, reading them in publication order will help you see how Sir Arthur Conan Doyle evolved as a writer, and some nuances and quirks of the canon are easier to notice if you take them in the same way that many readers did when the books were first published. Finally, these essays often build on and reference each other, so you may miss some nuance if you read them out of order, but I believe they should more or less hold up if you decide to jump around.

No matter what you do or how you read them, though, I hope this book helps you discover the same thrilling, maddening fascination with the world of Sherlock Holmes that I have. At the least, I hope it gives you something different to fight about on the Internet.

Themes, Elements, and Spoilers
There are a number of themes and elements that you should keep in mind as you read through the canon….

No, no. I hear you already. "*'Themes?'* *'Elements?'* This does not sound like an opinionated tour. This sounds like literature class! What have you tricked me into, Webb?"

Relax. All I really mean is that there are some common threads that run through Doyle's Holmes stories. When I started posting these essays on my blog, a few readers liked how I referenced the reoccurring bits that showed up in different stories, but they wanted to know what to look for at the start. That's all this is: a few suggestions of things to keep in mind as you read through the stories.

These themes and elements, however, may contain mild spoilers for the stories themselves, which leads me to another point. I am under the assumption that, after a hundred years, these stories are safely out of the spoiler zone, particularly things like the end of "The Final Problem" and the beginning of "The Empty House." If you really want to read the stories fresh for the first time and without spoilers, though, go ahead and read the story first before you read the accompanying essay. Seems pretty straightforward, but it's easy to get tripped up on these kinds of details when you're juggling nine different books.

Anyhow, those themes and elements I mentioned.

Continuity vs. Complexity: Watson's wound. Watson's wives. When Moriarty was first revealed. Doyle is notoriously bad about continuity within the canon, and finding all the errors can be entertaining or frustrating, depending on your inclinations. However, sometimes the more subtle conflicts are actually complexity of character rather than a flat-out mistake. Sherlockians are still arguing these points to this day.

11

Integration into Reality/History: Doyle tried to write his stories as if they really happened, by mentioning real-world events or previous cases as one connected universe. Indeed, that's part of the reason why Holmes was so popular in his time, and thus why the continuity errors are so jarring. Doyle really wanted Holmes to feel like a real person, and while the techniques Doyle used might sometimes come across as ham-fisted today, they were rarely (if ever) used in literature at the time. It's worth noting the little clues and details Doyle sprinkles into his stories.

Case Chronology: Doyle starts off presenting the cases in chronological order, but pretty soon he goes back and references earlier cases, and by the time you get halfway through the canon, any attempt to try and put the cases into chronological order becomes hopeless. This is a variation on the continuity errors, but it's a particular point that a lot of Sherlockians have tried to reconcile. However, there are distinct "eras" of Holmes' career: pre-Watson, pre-Watson's marriage, pre-Hiatus, post-Hiatus, and post-retirement. You may be surprised at how infrequently the structure of "two bachelors living together in Baker Street" (i.e., pre-Watson's marriage and possibly post-Hiatus) is actually used.

Unreliable Narrator: Aspects of the previous points can sometimes be chalked up to Watson being an unreliable narrator. An "unreliable narrator" is a literary device based on the fact that stories told from a first-person perspective are assumed to be completely accurate in the details they present to the reader — unreliable narrators, therefore, are… well, unreliable. Some Sherlockians have presented the case that Watson is an unreliable narrator, and certainly the Nigel Bruce interpretation of Watson as a bumbling, forgetful old fool (particular in the Basil Rathbone movies) gives some credibility to this theory. I tend to lean the other direction: Watson underplays his own talents to make his friend look better. Either way, Watson's level of reliability is something to keep in mind as you read.

Character Mythology vs. Canonical Representation: Sherlock Holmes and Dr. Watson are two of the most iconic characters in literature, and yet many people have utterly incorrect ideas of who these characters really are. The first couple of novels do a lot to present different characters than you might expect, but throughout the stories various little bits and details add up. You may find at the end of the canon that you really didn't know Holmes and Watson at all.

The Extended Cast: While not quite as famous, there are still characters associated with Holmes and Watson that are just as entrenched in popular culture: Mrs. Hudson, Inspector Lestrade, Wiggins, the Baker Street Irregulars, and Professor Moriarty, for example. Keep a careful eye out for them as well, as they aren't as prominent in the canon as you might expect. Particularly, note the large number of Scotland Yard inspectors that Holmes works with aside from Lestrade, and the wide variety of criminal masterminds he goes up against.

Science vs. Superstition: Perhaps the most defining theme of the Sherlock Holmes stories, and to an extent Victorian England as a whole. There are stories where Holmes directly confronts superstition, such as *The Hound of the Baskervilles* and "The Sussex Vampire," but he confronts minor superstitions in many of the stories, as well as biases, stereotypes, and assumptions. And as much as Holmes would like to think otherwise, once in a while he falls prey to such sloppy thinking as well. It is hard for him to work completely outside of the culture he is a part of.

Other Running Elements: Drug use (which shows up more or less than you would expect, depending on which depiction of Holmes you are used to), the occasional appearance of Billy the page, Holmes' complex relationship with women, and dozens of other elements pop up over and over throughout the canon. I'll try to point out the more interesting ones as they come up.

The Great Game

One last thing before we start our tour. Since I'll be referencing a few outside sources as we go, I should explain a bit about a strange quirk in the nature of research in the world of Sherlock Holmes.

Go to any website for fans of a popular property. Check out the scale of fan fiction written about the property. Look at all the arguments, conflicts, and endless discussions of extremely minor points of the canon. Dig into the wide range of fan approaches to it, from positively academic to utterly insane. Extrapolate that to a fandom lasting well over a century, and you start to get a sense of the sheer scale of Sherlock Holmes fandom. Before there was an Internet, radio, or even much mass media beyond publication, Sherlock Holmes fans were writing stories about the Holmes' "missing cases" or arguing about the nature of Watson's war wound. Fans all over the world corresponded with each other (and with Doyle), wrote to periodicals, started their own organizations and publications, created fan fiction, and even violated Arthur Conan Doyle's copyright — all the hallmarks of modern fandom. If there was a medium invented between the late

19th century and now, someone has probably used it to write a Holmes pastiche or give their opinions about something in the canon.

For the moment, let's look at just the analytical portions of this — the "scholarship" if you will, which is often called "Sherlockiana" (with the scholars referred to as "Sherlockians"). The sheer volume of words spent discussing the Great Detective and his companion over the decades is staggering and impossible to accurately know, but beyond sheer size, there's an additional factor to keep in mind when reading through any of it: the conceit that Watson and Holmes were real people, or what is colloquially called "the Great Game." A lot of Sherlockian material is written from the viewpoint that Watson was a real person transcribing actual events, instead of being a fictional conceit to frame the stories of Sir Arthur Conan Doyle's imagination. As a result, not only are these fans trying to reconcile inaccuracies and conflicts within the fictional world presented within the stories, but they're also trying to reconcile them within established real world and historical facts as well!

As much as I adore the idea of the Great Game, I won't be playing it for this tour. All my discussion will come from the perspective that Sir Arthur Conan Doyle was the author of fictional stories that starred Dr. John Watson and Sherlock Holmes as protagonists. Further, I will be touching on only a percentage of a fraction of a *sliver* of the Sherlockian scholarship and pastiches out there, and only when I think they're interesting, rather than out of any misplaced feeling of being objective.

If you are the kind of fan that feels loves the idea of a lot of outside material to dig into and explore, Holmes fandom is a great place for it. If you want a far more detailed examination of the canon from within the conceit of the Great Game, buy *The New Annotated Sherlock Holmes* by Leslie S. Klinger. This collection was a huge inspiration for me and a valuable reference during my work on these essays. It's expensive, but it is worth every penny.

Every. Goddamned. Penny.

However, you don't need any of it to appreciate Sherlock Holmes. This is just a cautionary note that if you do explore outside the confines of this book, read each source carefully to determine if they're playing the Great Game or not, as that will have an impact on what you're reading.

A Study in Scarlet (1887)

Since these essays discuss the plot points of each story by necessity, I encourage you to read them after you've read the story in question, as they will contain spoilers. Of course, now that I've said that, I'm going to immediately suggest something about *A Study in Scarlet* before you read it. It's only half of a Sherlock Holmes novel, and a slim novel overall, but you can skip chapters one through five of the second part and not miss much of anything. Look up that section of the plot on Wikipedia, or read it if you really want the whole experience, but know going in that I'm going to skip lightly over a chunk of this book.

But don't worry — I'll make it up to you. This is the very first Sherlock Holmes story, so there's a lot of groundwork to establish Watson and Holmes as characters before the case begins in earnest, and I have a lot of opinions about the early portion of the book. Really, even if you decide you don't want to go over the entire canon, reading just the first two chapters of *Scarlet* tells you a lot about the two characters that dispels quite a number of myths and misconceptions about them (as well as introducing a number of controversies down the road, as you'll see).

Dr. John Watson

Ah, Watson. One of the most misunderstood and misrepresented characters in the entire Holmes mythology. The injustices that popular culture have heaped upon Watson are multiple and horrid. If there is one thing I want to beat into the minds of every person who thinks they know something about Sherlock Holmes, it's that *Watson is not a bumbling, passive idiot*. After a few pages of *Scarlet*, we learn that he's a medical doctor and has served in the military. He's incredibly good at noticing details, such as in chapter five when he rattles off a number of sound observations, even if his deductions are off. He also frequently makes good perceptions regarding the character of people throughout the canon (at least, the male characters — he's a bit of a ladies' man, as we'll learn in *The Sign of the Four*). He's clearly not on Holmes' level as a detective, but even Holmes sometimes calls Watson's observations "invaluable" and, occasionally, it's not even sarcastic.

These first two chapters do a lot to dispel the mythical Stupid Passive Watson. Watson's conversation with Stamford demonstrates that Holmes has difficulty making friends with people, and yet Watson manages it pretty quickly after meeting him. Watson challenges Holmes in chapter two, flat-out chastising him for his lack of knowledge of the solar system. (Granted, later stories put this lack of knowledge into doubt, but it still shows Watson's strength of character that he's willing to butt heads with Holmes.) He even notices Holmes "being addicted to the use of some narcotic" just by watching him lie on the couch. If anything, Watson is guilty of not trusting his own capabilities — he discounts his observation of Holmes' addiction in the same scene.

As we enter the story, Watson has been shot in military action in Afghanistan. He explicitly mentions being shot in the shoulder, and the conversation in chapter two clarifies that it's the left shoulder. Make a note of this — it will come up later in one of the most notoriously debated details in the canon. (In fact, it's so notorious that it's actually a point of mockery in some parodies of Holmes.) Regardless, some point to Watson's passivity in this novel as a common sign of his character, and some portrayals of Watson seem to come from the actor having read the first chapter of *Scarlet* before throwing the rest of the book into the fire and jumping in front of the camera to act like a complete imbecile. The war wound shows that this isn't the case: he's recovering from a debilitating illness, one that caused him to be shipped out of action on very short notice. Watson even confesses that he becomes lazy when he's ill, and that he has "other vices" when he's well. We'll learn about those other vices in later stories, but the key point here is that he's *injured*. I haven't been shot before, but I expect if I was, I damn well wouldn't be keen on running around the city and trying to exercise my mental powers for subtle observation. Even after having minor outpatient surgery, all I want to do is lie on the couch and watch TV. Accusing Watson for being lazy because he's recovering from a bullet wound is damned cruel, and all of popular culture should be ashamed of itself.

One interesting thing I noticed on my rereading *Scarlet* is that Watson actually doesn't like London that much when he first gets there, referring to it as "that great cesspool." Watson is there only because of his disability, and Holmes only because it is the best place to practice his new profession — their romantic attachment to London develops over the course of the canon (and in Watson's case, never really forms — later stories make it clear he prefers the country). Also, Watson mentions that he keeps a "bull pup," but that detail never comes up again. It might refer to his service revolver and not a dog, but either way, it only comes up this one time. This reference does explain the appearance of a bulldog in Holmes and Watson's flat in the Guy Ritchie films, though, and reinforces my opinion that the team on those films was actually very aware of the canon (even if I personally feel the second one loses the thread).

The conversation with Stamford brings up a key point that will come up over and over again in the canon — the conflict of superstition and science in Victorian England. Stamford refers to Holmes as being too "cold-blooded" for his tastes, and ties it to Holmes' scientific mind and inclination, as if those who are *not* scientifically minded are more approachable and human. The fact that a doctor can hold this contradictory viewpoint of science being beneficial and yet damaging to someone's character is very Victorian — science is good to have, but too much of it is scary and potentially dangerous. One extreme (and well-known) example comes up in *Dr. Jekyll and Mr. Hyde,* but it is common in other "scientific romances" of the era.

This point is writ large in stories like *The Hound of the Baskervilles* and "The Sussex Vampire" (as well as in pastiches like *The Italian Secretary* by Caleb Carr), but you'll see notes of it over and over again throughout the canon. Doyle himself became more inclined toward the Spiritualism movement as he grew older, but his stories constantly have Holmes battling superstition. This conflict is a key part of Watson's character: he is both a man of science and a man that worries about what science is doing to humanity. He constantly straddles this line as a doctor and as a soldier who has seen terrible things in his life — he wants to believe in Holmes' rational world, but sometimes he can't help regressing to superstitious thoughts. That doesn't make him an idiot; it just makes him a man in Victorian England.

Mr. Sherlock Holmes

Much like how many assume that Watson is an idiot, people also assume that Holmes is some kind of super-genius that knows everything. To be fair, he's often written that way in a variety of pastiches (and, to an extent, by Doyle himself), but it's still not entirely true. Once Watson and Holmes are settled into 221B, Watson becomes obsessed with Holmes and writes a list of what Holmes does and doesn't know, as well as what he can do and cannot do. Many points of this list turn out to be completely wrong — I generally take this to mean that Watson doesn't know Holmes as much as he thinks he does, although some of it can certainly be laid at the feet of Doyle's legendary continuity errors — but there are some key points that will resonate throughout the canon. (As a side note, Watson's obsession with Holmes in this scene is one of the little bits in the canon that have fueled the "Watson is gay for Holmes and vice versa" theories for decades. And you thought it all started with Kirk and Spock.)

In fact, this list leads to one of my favorite scenes in the novel, the "brain-attic" speech where Holmes explains that knowledge of how the Earth rotates around the sun is completely irrelevant to him, and how he will try to forget it as soon as possible. I loved this scene as a kid because the idea of learning only what you need to know and nothing else made sense to me (although that logic drove my teachers mad), but as an adult I love it because it shows how Holmes is so quick to impress his new friend that he ends up taking perfectly sound theories and going just a little too far with them. I have personally gone back and forth, for example, on how much knowledge of art and going to the theater really related to the science of deduction — on the one hand, art does inspire crime, and Holmes has certainly used disguise and stagecraft to help him in his investigations, but on the other hand his encyclopedic knowledge of popular music of the time seems out of place with his own "brain-attic" theory. With careful reading, it's clear that Holmes has developed a series of quotable maxims for his newly-developing science (and *Scarlet* has one of my favorites: "It is a capital mistake to theorize before you have all the evidence"), but he isn't as perfect a practitioner of them as he thinks his is, or perhaps as much as he wants to be. It's one of the things that make him such a fascinating character.

Let's look back at Watson's list, so I can rant on another point about Holmes. One of the biggest criticisms I've heard about Robert Downey Jr.'s version of Holmes in the Guy Ritchie films was that Holmes wasn't a fighter. That's just plain wrong — Watson clearly lists Holmes as being an "expert singlestick player, boxer, and swordsman," and this is not the only time it comes up in the canon. Granted, Watson is handier with a gun than Holmes is, but Holmes is by no means a shrinking violet or a sickly man living only in his mind — he is a formidable combatant in his own right. If anything, Watson's military experience only seems to be helpful later in their career — with Holmes' fitness and Watson's illness at this early stage, Holmes is the more dangerous of the two. Personally, I believe the misconception came when Holmes was popular on the radio — it was very hard to portray action in radio drama, so over time those elements were minimized, and later interpretations of the character used the radio version as a basis.

Another commonly misunderstood point is his actual job. Holmes is not a private detective, and certainly not the first detective. Setting aside Auguste Dupin predating Holmes (more on that in a moment), in *Scarlet* Holmes mentions that he is neither a government detective nor a private detective, implying that others of both stripes existed before him. Rather, he is a consulting detective, giving advice to both direct clients and other detectives, and only going to the scene of the crime when the case is particularly difficult or interesting. It's an understandably misunderstood point, though, because over time Holmes does take on more and more direct commissions, and becomes a private detective in deed, if not in name. But in his pre-Watson career, Holmes solves most of his cases in his sitting room.

Finally, Doyle plants the seeds for the Great Game in these first two chapters. Not only do we have the conceit that Watson is transcribing actual events in his journal, but Holmes also disparages two detectives that predate him — C. Auguste Dupin, who was created by Edger Allen Poe, and Monsieur Lecoq, written by Emile Gaboriau. Referring to other writer's detectives caused many people to believe that Sherlock Holmes was real, even if Holmes did come down hard on his predecessors. Interestingly, Holmes disparages Dupin's "trick of breaking in on his friends' thoughts," but it is something that Holmes himself will do in future stories — again, Holmes' words do not always match up with his deeds.

The Minor Characters

Some of the more notable minor characters are also introduced in this novel, including the infamous Inspector G. Lestrade. One of controversial aspects of Lestrade is how to pronounce his name. I have heard it pronounced "Leh-strahde" and "Leh-strayed." (I tend to go with "Leh-strahde," personally.) Like Watson, Lestrade is often presented as an imbecile, although Holmes explicitly says he is "the best of a bad lot." Over the canon, however, we learn that Lestrade is actually quite an accomplished detective in his own right, and that his frequent conflicts with Holmes are tempered by a prickly loyalty to him. Sadly, he does become more of an idiot, which is unfortunate because here you can see some of the complexities of the character that get lost in the later canon, as well as in many adaptations and pastiches. (For my money, the best Inspector

Lestrade was portrayed by Colin Jeavons in the 1984 Granada television series.)

In this story, we also meet Detective Gregson, and find out that Gregson and Lestrade are rivals. This is functionally irrelevant, because throughout the canon Lestrade ends up the de facto winner of the rivalry, taking the lion's share of the police role in later stories. Lestrade is actually much quicker to admit his limitations than Gregson was, and he's the only police officer mentioned who consults Holmes prior to Watson's regular involvement with the cases. Further, at the murder scene for Enoch Drebber, Lestrade makes a number of good observations, and is even the one who finds the word "Rache," which Holmes might have missed otherwise. Sure, it's a red herring, but it does add information to Holmes' description of the murderer. Like I said — Lestrade's got more going on than most people realize.

The scene with Constable Rance is noteworthy for three things. One of the smaller points is that it demonstrates Holmes' willingness to bribe people for information — we see that while Holmes can deduce information from looking at someone, he's willing to use any means necessary to get data (although later he relies more and more on purely observational deduction). We also see the conflict of superstition and reason again, as Rance admits that was afraid of ghosts, although "nothing this side of the grave" scared him otherwise. Finally, Holmes will (in later stories) mock Watson for his florid turns of phrase, but it's Holmes himself that waxes poetic about this case, and even gives it the name "a study in scarlet."

Mrs. Hudson appears in this novel, although she's never referred to by name — only as "the landlady." Wiggins also appears, as well as Holmes' "army of street Arabs." And so, many of the key secondary characters all make their first appearance in this novel... even Watson's trusty service revolver.

Oh God, the Mormons

At the halfway point, the book turns into a completely different story, with no explanation before or after. It's not a section written by Dr. Watson, or indeed by any other character. As a story in and of itself, it's not bad, even if the Mormons are woefully misinterpreted. But think about it — to Doyle, 1880s America was about as foreign to him as Victorian England is to us. He was going on what stories and news he had heard, which was all sensationalism and glorified lies. It's awkward reading it in modern times, but taken just as a story, it switches between lines of brilliance ("did God make this country?") and terrible jumps in logic (John Ferrier isn't afraid of anything... except numbers). It's really just a completely different novel smashed into the middle, which Jefferson Hope then explains in part two, chapter six anyhow!

Between the time I wrote my original essays on *Scarlet* and the time I was preparing this book for publication, there was a news article in *The Daily Progress* about how the book was removed from six-grade reading lists in Charlottesville, Virginia because it was "derogatory toward Mormons." Let's put aside whether a murder mystery is age-appropriate to begin with, because clearly it was banned for the Mormon section. If anything, though, that's even *more* reason why it needs to be read. *Scarlet* is a perfect example of what happens when people work from ignorance. Doyle's later stories about America were much more respectful after he went on a tour of America (and certainly after American sales helped to increase his profits). Comparing and contrasting *A Study in Scarlet* with *The Valley of Fear* might be useful in showing the difference in outside perceptions of American culture, as well as showing what it's like when the media grossly stereotypes a particular religious group — certainly a valid discussion for the modern day.

But aside from all that, the second half of the book just isn't a Sherlock Holmes story, and the bits that are about Holmes aren't great. The book is a vital a part of the canon, though, and there are key scenes that are so impactful that they are a part of my very makeup. I always start any reread of the canon with *Scarlet*, and every time I am thrilled to explore the canon's genesis, even if the execution frustrates me.

The Sign of the Four (1890)

Watson and Holmes

On to the second Holmes story, where points go to Watson right off the bat. Up front, page one, we get to see the drug habit that was only alluded to in *Scarlet*: Holmes uses a "seven-per-cent solution" of cocaine to keep his mind from stagnating when he is not engaged on a case. This on-again, off-again (and, in Victorian times, *entirely legal*) drug use is one of the many misconceptions about the Great Detective. Before Nicholas Meyer's fantastic pastiche *The Seven-Percent Solution*, it was never mentioned at all in pop culture depictions of Holmes. Since then, the topic has been portrayed extremely inconsistently. Perhaps the most unusual example of divergence from the canon is the Granada television series, where Jeremy Brett's Holmes actually kicks the habit due to the series getting complaints about drug use on television. (Up to that point, the show's Holmes had been portrayed pretty close to how the original stories were written). The most extreme example of drug abuse, however, is probably Hugh Laurie's portrayal of Gregory House on *House, M.D.* Though *House* is not technically a Holmes pastiche, there's so much obvious inspiration drawn between Gregory House and Sherlock Holmes that it's bled back over into other portrayals of Holmes over the past decade — a strange case of a Holmes-inspired character cycling back to inspire portrayals of Holmes.

Back to Watson. A key part of understanding him is the line "... my conscience swelled nightly within me...." Watson is Holmes' conscience in many ways, constantly questioning and challenging not only Holmes' deductions but his motives, and the dialogue in the early chapters of the novel attests to that. Notice how Watson encourages Holmes to deduce and exercise his brain, just to keep him from turning back to the needle. Yet, when Watson announces his intention to marry, it is to the needle that Holmes returns — Watson, his conscience, has fled him. From one book to the next, the relationship between the men has changed and grown — far from the unchanging, staid relationship we see in various adaptations (or, to be fair, in the middle part of Doyle's canon).

Watson's wound is now in his leg. In fact, Doyle has decided so completely that the wound is in Watson's leg that the point is brought up at least three times during the course of the novel, even though it was clearly his left shoulder in *Scarlet*. I expect Doyle was called on this, because the balance of the canon keeps it vaguely referred to as "my wound" or "the wound in my limb." Also, Watson still claims he is recovering from his illness sustained in Afghanistan, even though it's explicitly after the events in *Scarlet* (and, we learn in later stories, several years after their meeting). Thus here we are, only two stories into the canon, and already there are errors in continuity. Get used to this, gentle reader — you will see me rant about Doyle's inaccuracies many times before we are through.

Another attempt by Doyle to break down the divide between fiction and reality is to have Holmes refer to the previous novel and comment upon it, even if it does introduce problems in chronology later. As Watson defends his publication of *Scarlet*, Holmes chides him for his "romanticism," even though it was Holmes who poetically named the case! It's possible that this is another continuity error, but I prefer to think that Holmes has just conveniently rewritten the incident in his mind — something that he has done a couple of times already.

We also learn, through Holmes' deduction of Watson's pocket watch, the reason why Watson has "no kith and kin in England": both his father and his elder brother are dead. Both men had the first initial H., and popular Sherlockian lore calls them Henry Sr. and Jr., although the canon never addresses the point directly.

Finally, Watson is quite the ladies' man. Not only does he remark on his "experience of women which extends over many nations and three separate continents," but Mary is clearly flirting with Watson shortly after their introduction. Watson is very taken by her as well, although either his emotions or his illness cause him to make several mistakes throughout the story as a result. Watson also ends up engaged, which opens up another infamous Watson continuity snarl — his married life. Despite his shortcomings, Watson's relationship with Mary shows is that he is not the fat, overblown buffoon portrayed by Nigel Bruce. (Oh, Nigel Bruce, you have so much to answer for.)

Holmes at one point says "It is simplicity itself," which reminds me of another peeve I have about misconceptions of the canon. Holmes does refer to things as "elementary," and he does say such things to Watson, but he never uses the phrase "Elementary, my dear Watson." Not once. Where it actually comes from or when it became popular is a bit of a muddle, but signs point to the William Gillette play *Sherlock Holmes,* which premiered in 1899. What makes it more confusing is that Conan Doyle did write an early draft of that play before William Gillette rewrote it, so some argue for the play being part of the "extended canon," but since the play is rewritten from three other stories and takes drastic liberties with the characters, as well as Doyle's overall apathy towards the whole production, I consider it an adaptation at best.

We also see more in this story of Holmes' snobbery. He laments that crime in London and existence as a whole is "commonplace," and how he can't abide the commonplace. We also see his sense of humor. After chiding Watson for his lack of observation, Watson remarks on Mary Morstan being beautiful. Holmes' reply is "Is she? I did not observe." Finally, Holmes demonstrates his opinion of women quite clearly. "Women are never to be entirely trusted — not the best of them." This will come into play in the very next story.

Other Points

We learn that this case is set in 1888, based on Mary's story (which causes *lots* of problems later). However, Watson and Holmes have been rooming together for "years," so *Scarlet* is likely set before its 1887 publication date.

To touch back on an earlier rant about Holmes being good at fighting, the conversation with McMurdo reinforces Holmes' aptitude with boxing and fists. Further, McMurdo mentions that his bout with Holmes was "four years back," which means it was in 1884. It's possible that, since Holmes was entertaining clients before he moved to 221B Baker Street, he may have been boxing after he started his career as a consulting detective.

This story has another famous axiom of Holmes': "How often have I said to you that when you have eliminated the impossible, whatever remains, however impossible, must be the truth?"

Four also introduces Toby, the amazing tracking mongrel. As a kid, I had a soft spot for Toby because of his expanded role in *The Great Mouse Detective*. Granted, in the movie Toby is Holmes' pet, but whatever. Toby is awesome, even if he only shows up for one story, and I'll fight anyone who says otherwise.

Mrs. Hudson gets named in this story, but the maid that was mentioned in passing in *Scarlet* seems to have disappeared. But the Baker Street Irregulars get their name, so it all works out.

Doyle's Style

Sign of the Four was written three years after *Scarlet*, and there's a noticeable difference in Doyle's style — the most noteworthy being a firmer adherence to the conceit of being Watson's memoirs. Further, it's very different from a lot of Victorian literature and other serialized storytellers of the time, like Dickens. The opening is positively modern, dropping you right into a dramatic situation between Holmes and Watson. The rest of the novel is well-paced as well — even during lengthy expositions (of which there are several), Doyle works in little quirks and ticks of character to keep the reader engaged. This style of writing is one of the many reasons why the stories still hold up today.

Doyle also has a penchant for eccentric characters — all the Sholtos ooze quirky fun, and even the presence of the dead ones are felt through the course of the story through the stories and anecdotes of the other characters. There's also a boat chase near the end, and Holmes demonstrates his famous mastery of disguise. Doyle is, at heart, an adventure writer, and there's plenty of it in this novel.

Doyle also uses the contrivance of "nested stories," where one character tells a story that another character narrates. Obviously, Watson is one character, and he transcribes the narration of other characters. But at one point, Sholto himself narrates another character's story. This is a really hard thing to pull off, and yet Doyle does so to great effect in this book (and indeed, in many of his stories).

On the other hand, with this story we do run into some of the prejudices of the age. Strange Oriental treasures are just the top of the list of awkward stereotypes. Manipulative Indians and blood-thirsty black savages abound in this story. To be fair, Doyle is no Sax Rohmer or H.P. Lovecraft — it is possible to read this story and see these characters are merely bad examples of their various cultures. But it certainly skirts the comfort zone of modern sensibilities.

And, sadly, Doyle does have his moments of being positively overwrought:

He pointed to what looked like a long dark thorn stuck in the skin just above the ear.

"It looks like a thorn," said I.

"It is a thorn..."

The Adventures of Sherlock Holmes

A Scandal in Bohemia (1891)

Now we start with the first book of short stories, and the very first story is one of my favorites (as well as Doyle's) — "A Scandal in Bohemia." One of the reasons why this story is so fondly remembered is because of Irene Adler, or "The Woman" as Holmes calls her. Compare Holmes' rather glowing opinion of Adler here to his generally low opinions of women in the previous stories. Despite Watson's protestations that Holmes is devoid of emotion, it's clear that this isn't the case. Sadly, before we meet the woman that Watson mysteriously refers to as "the late Irene Adler" (even though she doesn't die in the course of this story), we run into more continuity snags.

Watson is married by the time this story starts. He mentions reading at least three of Holmes' cases in the paper, has put on seven and a half pounds since he last met Holmes, and has become nostalgic for his time in 221B. And yet, the story clearly starts on March 20th, 1888, which is a few months *before* he met Mary! This has led some Sherlockians to claim that *The Sign of the Four* is actually set in the middle of 1887, but it's still less than a year for an engagement, a marriage, a move into a new home, establishing a new medical practice, and the hiring of a new servant girl. Others have pointed to the fact that Mary isn't mentioned by name, and therefore Watson is referring to a second wife, one he had before he met Mary. Personally, I figure Doyle probably meant that the story is set in 1889, but don't worry — the chronology of the stories gets even worse as we go deeper. This doesn't touch on other errors, like why Mrs. Hudson is suddenly changed into "Mrs. Turner." Poor Mrs. Hudson.

This story also has some of my favorite bits in the canon, like "you see but you do not observe" and "It is a capital mistake to theorize before one has data." This is also the case where Holmes mentions there are seventeen steps leading up to their rooms, a detail which I noted during the Introduction as having such a bizarrely influential role in my youth. There's also the scene where Holmes relates his efforts in following Irene Adler in disguise, only to get coerced into being the best man at her secret wedding.

There's some good Watson watching here. For the third time, Watson tries to excuse himself from Holmes' client, and Holmes insists he stay. It speaks to Watson's sense of propriety (although, you'd think by this point he'd be more comfortable acting as Holmes' assistant), as does his discomfort and shame at being instructed to act against the "beautiful creature" that tended to Holmes. We also learn of Watson's strong sense of justice — he's willing to break the law and risk arrest in the name of a good cause. Finally, Watson's simple statement of "Then you may entirely rely on me" is a powerful statement of his loyalty to Holmes. This is a huge deal, as this is the first story where Watson takes an active part in the case, instead of merely reporting the facts.

As mentioned previously, Holmes continues to make it clear his opinion that women are "naturally secretive," and is initially shocked when Adler outsmarts him. His misogyny has backfired on him, and while his ego is bruised, he clearly respects Adler's outmaneuvering him, and his opinion on women as a whole seems to have evolved. We also learn that Holmes likes to have trophies of his cases (or at least his most interesting ones), regardless of the outcome. We'll see these trophies again in later stories.

Interestingly, as influential as Adler is in the canon and to Holmes, we don't see much of her directly. All we learn of her is second-hand, with the exception of one conversation and a letter she writes to Holmes. Further, although Watson claims that Holmes called her "The Woman" afterwards, in fact whenever Holmes (rarely) mentions her in later stories, it's always as "Irene Adler." In the end, she's barely a blip in the overall canon, less impactful than Inspector Gregson. However, even her light touch on the life of Sherlock Holmes is enough to enshrine her in his mind, and in the canon as a whole.

The Adventure of the Red-Headed League (1891)

We move on to another favorite story of Doyle's, "The Red-Headed League." I always found this story to be a touch overcomplicated — not in the delivery, but in the means by which the perpetrators go about their crime. One of my friends has suggested to me that the overcomplication is intentional humor on Doyle's part, which is a direction I hadn't considered before. Either way, I like the fact that it's a Victorian-era con game, and a story that includes the introduction (and subsequent arrest) of an intelligent thief, the "fourth-smartest man in London." It's a good example of a Sherlock Holmes story that doesn't involve a murder, and for that I think it makes a good read, and one of my personal top ten. (If nothing else, it also shows that British prejudice against gingers was alive and well in the Victorian era.)

This story has the introduction of another police agent: Peter Jones (or, perhaps, it's another appearance by Athelney Jones — there are certainly a number of similarities between the two). Watson is still trying to excuse himself from the sitting room when Holmes sees his clients. We are witness to the first of a number of night watches with Holmes and Watson, and the only time the two of them use the London Underground. This is the first time that Holmes calls a case "unique," as well as being the origin of the phrase "a three-pipe problem." We find out that Holmes is quite the card player. We also find the first bit of continuity that's established before a later story features it — in this case, it's a reference to Miss Mary Sutherland, who is Holmes' client in "A Case of Identity."

We also get an interesting peek into Watson's mindset. His observation of Mr. Jabez Wilson runs as follows:

Our visitor bore every mark of being an average commonplace British tradesman, obese, pompous, and slow.

In interpretations of the canon, Watson is often portrayed as obese, pompous, and slow (in particular, the Nigel Bruce interpretation of him), but in the canon, we see that Watson is actually a bit snobbish of the more blue-collar clients Holmes sometimes has.

We have another continuity error. Doing a bit of rudimentary math, the story is set in June 1890 (April is "two months ago," according to Watson), but the note disbanding the Red-Headed League is dated October 1890. Two references support the idea that it's June 1890, so I tend to go with that. Watson also calls on Holmes instead of being present in 221B, so we can also assume that this case is equally post-marriage, just like "A Scandal in Bohemia."

Sadly, John Clay doesn't appear in the canon again, although some people retroactively make John Clay a part of

Moriarty's gang. Personally, and based on pure audacity and long-term planning, I'd probably put John Clay on the level of Arsène Lupin. (If you don't know who Arsène Lupin is, that's a whole different series of essays....)

A Case of Identity (1891)

Like *A Study in Scarlet*, this is a case in which no actual crime has been committed, but there's a lot going on under the surface.

This story is the first of many jumps backwards in continuity. The client in this case is Miss Mary Sutherland, who was mentioned in the previous story, "The Red-Headed League," although the reference to the gift from the King of Bohemia implies it takes place after "A Scandal in Bohemia." For the first time, Watson *doesn't* excuse himself from listening to the client's woes. I'm inclined to think that Watson is more likely to remain present when a woman's honor is challenged, but it could just as easily be chalked up to another continuity error.

In this story, we first hear of "the boy in buttons" at the Baker Street residence. I admit that I didn't remember any page in the canon, but he's absolutely there, and we'll see him again. I've also noticed a regular thread to Holmes' adages about the importance of minutiae. This time, it's "It has long been an axiom of mine that the little things are infinitely the most important." It's certainly a key part of Holmes' process.

This is also the first time we see Holmes' willingness to take justice into his own hands, as with his explosive confrontation with James Windibank. This comes up again in the next story as well ("The Boscombe Valley Mystery"). On a first read-through, it might seem that Holmes is merely trying to scare

Windibank, but combined with the next story, we get a very real sense that Holmes has his own code of justice that doesn't always match up with the ideas of the legal system.

One interesting scene is when Holmes asks Watson to recount his observations of Miss Sutherland. Watson proceeds to do so, and Holmes makes the following remark:

"'Pon my word, Watson, you are coming along wonderfully. You have really done very well indeed. It is true that you have missed everything of importance, but you have hit upon the method, and you have a quick eye for color."

Yes, Holmes is mocking Watson here, but he is also complimenting Watson, and perhaps elevating him over the regular cast of New Scotland Yard detectives that come through the door of 221B. It's another indication of Watson's intelligence, as well as Holmes' growing respect for him.

As for the case itself, every time I read it I find it more and more frustrating. Not the details of the case — Holmes makes some excellent observations about typewriters and costuming which show that his craft is more than measuring footprints and studying cigar ash. It's not even the conduct of Mr. Windibank, which is creepy and utterly reprehensible but at least somewhat plausible, given the relatively small difference between his age and that of Mary Sutherland.

No, what gets me is that, every time I read it, I am more and more convinced that Mrs. Windibank had to have been involved with the scheme from the start. The idea that a woman would allow her husband to seduce her daughter just to keep her income makes Mrs. Windibank one of the lowest characters in the

Holmes canon, even though we never see her. Further, at one point Holmes says, "With the connivance and assistance of his wife...." To this, Mr. Windibank confirms, "*We* never thought that she would have been so carried away." (Emphasis mine.) Combined with the almost intentional blindness that Mary Sutherland has toward the true nature of the situation, I find it difficult to empathize with any of the Windibank family. Each time I read it, I hope that the whole family has something horrible happen to them.

The Boscombe Valley Mystery (1891)

In all the previous stories, Holmes gravitated to various key unusual details which helped him to solve the case. In "The Boscombe Valley Mystery," the case appears to be relatively straightforward to everyone except Holmes. It's also the first case which doesn't start in 221B Baker Street, and in which Holmes and Watson leave London entirely. But Lestrade comes back, and Holmes mentions his monograph on ash again, just in case you were thinking everything in this story was new.

In my head, I always confuse this story with *The Hound of the Baskervilles*. There are certainly a lot of common elements (such as the train ride, a period of separation between Watson and Holmes, and a murder in a remote part of England), but the stories are actually pretty distinct once you get into both of them. Still, if you've read this story with a sense of *déjà vu*, you're not the only one.

This is the first (and one of the few) times where Holmes is referenced to wearing a "close-fitting cloth cap." This is the infamous deerstalker (a style of rural hunting hat) that Holmes is often depicted as wearing, even though he almost never does. Seriously. It shows up once here, once in *Hound*, and once in

"Silver Blaze," and that's it. The rest of the time, he's wearing a top hat or other fashionable accessories more appropriate to the city. However, the artist at the time (Sidney Paget) drew Holmes wearing the cap, and it became such an iconic reference that it ended up being the character's trademark.

But really, he barely wears the damn thing.

Holmes is well known for his ability to make deductions based on physical cues, but this story has a good example of Holmes working from psychological evidence: his doubts about the case all start from the fact that James McCarthy is unsurprised by his arrest, even though he claims to be innocent. Holmes' logic is sound as he explains it to Watson, but it shows the logical and reasoning Holmes working from the comfort of his room, rather than the energetic and excitable Holmes gathering evidence at the scene of the crime. We also get a good scene of Watson doing some deductions on his own, using his medical knowledge on the inquest while Holmes is away.

There's a short exchange in this story that I particular like:

I shook my head. "Many men have been hanged on far slighter evidence," I remarked.

"So they have. And many men have been wrongfully hanged."

There's also another good example of how deep their friendship has become, as Holmes uses Watson as a sounding board for his reasoning after a frustrating exchange with Lestrade.

As in the last story, we see Holmes taking the law into his own hands here. Whereas in "A Case of Identity" there wasn't a crime actually committed, but Holmes threatens to punish the villain anyhow, in this story the villain is quite clearly the guilty party, but Holmes withholds the evidence until a time he feels is correct. Holmes is becoming more and more convinced at this stage in his career of his own ability to mete out appropriate justice, instead of simply supporting the legal authorities.

This leads into another back-and-forth rant about the canon. As previously mentioned, the conceit of the stories are that they are actual events that Watson transcribes and publishes both as a form of advertisement for Holmes and as a way to demonstrate Holmes' amazing new science of deduction. At the end of this story, though, Watson quite clearly writes:

... and there is every prospect that the son and daughter may come to live happily together in ignorance of the black cloud which rests upon their past.

This is true, if they for some reason never pick up a copy of the *Strand* magazine in which the stories were originally published!

On the one hand, in later stories Watson explicitly mentions that he is falsifying and obfuscating names, locations, and details of some cases. In this story he doesn't mention that he's doing that, but the locations are false (as are many of the locations in previous cases), so it is at least implied that, were these real transcriptions of real cases, the facts would be sufficiently muddled. But why would Watson risk alienating a European king with even a disguised account of his former mistress, as in "A Scandal in Bohemia"? There are stories later in the canon with even more dire references, even through the lens of false details.

Ultimately, this is the reason why I don't often play the Great Game with my Holmes analysis. If we buy into the conceit that these were true cases, the details start to break down much more quickly, and the stories become an exercise in reconciling fact and fiction. By accepting it as a narrative device, though, I find that I can suspend my disbelief enough to accept that Watson would have published such an account even after promising never to tell anyone. (Frustratingly, even I can't suspend my disbelief enough to accept a story taking on a completely new narrator halfway through, such as with *A Study in Scarlet* — another reason that story leaves me so conflicted.) Other people feel that such a structure breaks down with each false note, jarring the reader out of the conceit every time it happens. Each reader has to make their own decision on it, although I suspect it gets easier to buy into the idea of blurring fact and fiction as the stories age and the London of the 19th century becomes a hazy memory in history.

The Five Orange Pips (1891)

Now we move on to a story where Holmes matches wits with the KKK (yes, *that* KKK), and nothing really happens. While this case lacks resolution, it provides some more key points that helps (and hinders) continuity.

For example, Watson makes a reference that he has been chronicling cases from 1882 to 1890, which heavily implies that *A Study in Scarlet* takes place around 1882. However, this case is set on September 1887, even though he claims he is still married and has a vague reference to Irene Adler. Since Watson appears to be reminiscing here, it's possible that he got the date wrong, but I'm more inclined to believe that this case is later than 1887.

In this story we also start getting references to the so-called "apocryphal cases," cases that Watson mentions in passing but are never written by Doyle himself. These little references have provided a lot of pastiche fodder over the decades (with mixed results), and we'll probably see more versions of these apocryphal cases by various authors for years to come.

More telling, though, is the fact that this story twice mentions multiple defeats of Holmes prior to 1890:

Some, too, have baffled his analytical skill, and would be, as narratives, beginnings without an ending...

and

"I have been beaten four times - three times by men, and once by a woman."

It helps to sell this particular unresolved case, and adds a whiff of authenticity — even the famous Sherlock Holmes can be, and has been, beaten and stymied.

There's also a great exchange that tells another small detail about the relationship between Holmes and Watson:

"Why," said I, glancing up at my companion, "that was surely the bell. Who could come to-night? Some friend of yours, perhaps?"

"Except yourself I have none," he answered.

There's also this:

We sat in silence for some minutes, Holmes more depressed and shaken than I had ever seen him.

Combine these with the fact that his vengeance against his fallen client contains a fair bit of bruised ego, and we see that Holmes is a far cry from the emotionless machine he claims to be!

We get more solid deductions from Watson about seaports and Texas, another appearance by the nameless maid, and the third story in a row where Holmes takes justice into his own hands. All signs point to this being a classic Holmes story.

That's not the case. Holmes' investigation ends up being a monologue, and the story just ends. Doyle tries to force a resolution by implying of the loss of the Lone Star, but in reality Holmes gets too cocky, his client dies, and he gets nowhere close to putting his hands on the culprits. We have yet another bloodthirsty American secret society that mysteriously has connections that reach into the heart of London. Maybe it's because of the similarities to the Mormons in *Scarlet*, or maybe because the strong impact it has on American culture, but I find it hard to get past the inclusion of the KKK in this story (even if the current KKK is actually a somewhat different organization founded in 1915). This story is an interesting attempt to try something new with the Holmes formula, but in my opinion it ends up being one of the weaker short stories.

The Man with the Twisted Lip (1891)

Now we come to a story about opium addiction and opium dens, that lurid darkness at the heart of prim and proper Victorian society. Opium dens were dirty, terrible places, but were perfectly legal for years — in fact, many people at the time didn't even think that opium was addictive. The scene with

Watson in the den trying to recover his friend is therefore surprisingly blunt, and Doyle (through Watson) doesn't flinch in his unrelenting opinions of these drug dens and the effects of opium on its users. One can inevitably draw a parallel between this den and Holmes' own addictions, and Holmes even remarks on it himself. In fact, if you carefully read through the scene, notice that Holmes doesn't actually deny using opium — he just implies that he isn't *now*. Given Holmes' propensity for wordplay, it's possible that the omission is intentional.

Aside from the opium den, though, this story is unusual in other ways. We're treated to a rare stretch of Watson's own independent adventuring, in which he proves to be as capable and forthright alone as he is with his friend, leaving on a moment's hesitation to go alone into a drug den to retrieve his patient. The story never once strays into Baker Street, and we get a glimpse into Watson's domestic life, something only implied or hinted at previously — although, again, Watson only refers to Mary as "my wife." He hasn't mentioned Mary's name since the story he met her!

The case centers on disguise. Although Holmes himself is in disguise only briefly (and, admittedly, his transformation for Watson borders a bit on the fantastic), his knowledge of stagecraft is instrumental in solving the case. We're also given some interesting details about the craft of disguise in the Victorian age. Many Sherlockians over the ages have considered the concept of a beggar making that much money to be unrealistic. However, recent studies have shown that panhandlers today can actually pull down quite a bit of money, so it's possible that Doyle was way ahead of his time.

We meet another policeman, Inspector Bradstreet, and learn that some of the men at Scotland Yard actually respect Holmes and his work. We also get another peek into Watson and Holmes' relationship:

> *"You have a grand gift of silence, Watson," said he. "It makes you quite invaluable as a companion. 'Pon my word, it is a great thing for me to have someone to talk to, for my own thoughts are not over-pleasant."*

There's a scene that sits weirdly with me, however. When Holmes is talking with Mary St. Clair, and she is convinced that her husband is still alive, based on her intuition. Holmes responds with:

> *"I have seen too much not to know that the impression of a woman may be more valuable than the conclusion of an analytical reasoner. And in this letter you certainly have a very strong piece of evidence to corroborate your view."*

If Holmes is serious, he's admitting that women's intuition is actually a valid tool in investigation, which seems contrary to every axiom he's mentioned thus far (and to his largely low opinion of women). I'm more inclined to think he's being sarcastic here, but if so, it's a very subtle indication of his frustration with her. However, he solves the mystery by making a pillow fort and smoking a lot, so I could argue that Holmes is certainly playing the eccentric in this story.

I've mentioned a lot of continuity controversies in the canon so far, but this story contains one that gets a lot of play in the Sherlockian community, and yet I don't think it's a big deal at all. It all stems from one line, spoken by Watson's wife:

"Now, you must have some wine and water, and sit here comfortably and tell us all about it. Or should you rather that I sent James off to bed?"

"James," here, is clearly a reference to Watson, introduced in *A Study in Scarlet* as Dr. *John* Watson. There has been a lot of discussion about who James is and how he figures into the canon — so much so that the topic warranted a separate article in *The New Annotated Sherlock Holmes, Vol. 1.* I always assumed that "James" was just a nickname for John. Everyone has their own opinions on what's controversial.

The Adventure of the Blue Carbuncle (1892)

Every Christmas, I run into images of the Victorian ideal of the holiday, a confluence of traditions and images that inevitably slides into renditions, quotes, and readings from *A Christmas Carol*. People hold up Scrooge and his ghosts as the most evocative story of the holiday season. But through my life, my favorite Christmas story hasn't been that Dickensian classic, but rather "The Adventure of the Blue Carbuncle." Other Sherlockians dismiss the story as one of the weaker cases in the book, but it has always held a special place in my heart, and I've read it dozens of times throughout my life. (I still notice little things each time I read it, though, like the fact that Holmes tends to crumple newspapers into a ball when he's done reading them.)

This case starts off with a scenario in which a crime isn't committed, and Watson specifically mentions three previous stories in which this is the case ("A Scandal in Bohemia," "A Case of Identity," and "The Man with the Twisted Lip"). Later we learn that there is a jewel theft, but it's another instance of Doyle drawing connections between his previous works and building an elaborate chronology around Holmes — even, as we've already seen, if it's fraught with inconsistencies and conflicts.

The scene in which Watson and Holmes analyze the hard-felt hat is perhaps one of my favorite scenes of deduction in the whole canon. Further, it's not only another example of Watson's own intelligence, but a clear instance of him downplaying his talent. Watson recounts a detailed list of observations (but not deductions) about the hat — a full paragraph of them. However, at the end, he says that he sees nothing. Even Holmes calls him "too timid" as a result!

As the case warms up, we meet another policeman — Peterson — and find another reference to Inspector Bradstreet. Holmes also puts in another advertisement in the paper as a key part of solving the case. In fact, many of Holmes' cases revolve around advertisements in the paper or short telegrams revealing a key fact. Even though mass media and instant communication was in its infancy by today's standards, Holmes used the technology available to him to great effect in acquiring details and trapping suspects. As a culture we have this image of Holmes that is quaint or antiquated, but in many ways Holmes was on the cutting edge of the intersection between technology and culture. He probably would have been absolutely in love with smartphones if he were around today (which the TV shows *Sherlock* and, to a lesser extent, *Elementary* demonstrate).

This story contains a great example of how manipulative Holmes can be. Far from being the unreasoning and unsocial machine that Holmes is sometimes perceived as, he can be quite adept at convincing people to reveal information about themselves, such as when Holmes masterfully manipulates Breckinridge into giving him information through his obsession with betting. (Gambling is something that pops up every now and then in the canon — something to keep an eye out for.)

The fascination with jewel thieves is actually quite common in the crime literature of the time — about as frequent as murder is in modern crime fiction — and is summed up perfectly by Holmes in this story:

> *"In the larger and older jewels every facet may stand for a bloody deed."*

Holmes once again takes justice into his own hands. Regardless of his good intentions, he lets a man who stole a valuable gem go without notifying the police, and explains that the puzzle is a major motivator for him, not the prosecution of criminals:

> *"Chance has put in our way a most singular and whimsical problem, and its solution is its own reward."*

All in all, it's an underrated story in the canon, and one of my personal favorites.

The Adventure of the Speckled Band (1892)

Although the image of Watson and Holmes rooming together as bachelors is prominent in our minds, this is only the second story thus far (out of ten) in the period between the two moving into 221B and Watson's marriage. We learn that this case is set in April 1883, so there's at least a four year gap between *A Study in Scarlet* (when Watson moved in, assuming this case took place shortly afterwards) and *The Sign of the Four* (when Watson proposed in 1887 or 1888). Even more interesting, Holmes makes a reference to a case before Watson boarded with him — a rare peek into Holmes' pre-Watson career.

As an earlier case, we see some of Watson and Holmes still learning the boundaries in their friendship. At one point, Holmes mentions a reluctance to include Watson due to the danger, and Watson very casually blows it off. Holmes doesn't think twice about endangering Watson in later cases (chronologically), but that's probably because the two of them have had conversations like this many times by that point.

We get to see some of Holmes' dry wit in the confrontation between him and Roylott:

"I know you, you scoundrel! I have heard of you before. You are Holmes, the meddler."

My friend smiled.

"Holmes, the busybody!"

His smile broadened.

"Holmes, the Scotland Yard Jack-in-office!"

Holmes chuckled heartily. "Your conversation is most entertaining," said he. "When you go out close the door, for there is a decided draught."

Some Victorian slang: a "Jack-in-office" is a rude, self-important, minor bureaucrat. Also, Holmes' reference earlier in the story to "knocking up" Watson, Mrs. Hudson, and himself means waking them up, not getting them pregnant. Just so you know.

We get another indication of Holmes' strength to consider in conjunction with the revelation of his boxing career back in *The Sign of the Four*; here, we watch Holmes unbend an iron poker with his bare hands. We have another long vigil in darkness. Holmes makes a reference to Watson's pistol as "Eley's No. 2," although I've always understood it to be a Webley. Doing some research, it turns out that Eley's was actually a manufacturer of *ammunition*, not firearms, and one of the models they made ammunition for was the Webley.

There's also a good example of Holmes observing someone's behavior and yet completely missing the emotion behind it (mistaking the shivers of fright for cold), reinforcing that Holmes just doesn't get women on some level:

"I am glad to see that Mrs. Hudson has had the good sense to light the fire. Pray draw up to it, and I shall order you a cup of hot coffee, for I observe that you are shivering."

In the end, this is an interesting case because the criminal is pretty obvious from the start — it's only the method of the murder that's in question. The revelation of the snake itself is controversial, since no such a snake exists in nature, and none of them has venom that kills in such a short timeframe. Also, there's a lot of speculation as to whether Holmes enacts his own justice again or is just the victim of an unfortunate accident, depending on whether you believe he knew the snake would go back and kill its owner. Still, it's one of Conan Doyle's favorite stories, and it's a great look into a period of the relationship between Holmes and Watson that is, at this point in the canon, still largely untouched.

The Adventure of the Engineer's Thumb (1892)

Right off the bat, Watson claims that this is only one of two cases that he brings to Holmes' attention — the other being the case of "Colonel Warburton's madness" (an apocryphal case). However, much later Watson does actually refer a third case to Holmes — he brings the concerns of an old school friend to Holmes' attention in "The Adventure of the Naval Treaty." While this isn't on the level of "Naval Treaty," though, it's still a fun story in its own right.

The story (or at least, the false story given to the client) revolves around fuller's earth. For years I always wondered why this was so valuable, so I looked into it. In the Victorian era, it was a kind of earth used for "industrial and medical purposes," according to *The New Annotated Sherlock Holmes*. Fuller's earth is still mined today, because it's used to absorb oils and grease in a number of areas of manufacture, including cloth production. There — now you've learned something unrelated to Holmes trivia.

One of the nuances of this story lost to modern readers is that engineers were very romantic figures. They were fairly rare in society — there's only one other engineer character in the canon — and they were often associated with exciting things like working on ships (naval fiction was akin to Westerns in terms of romanticism) and building bridges (which was precarious and dangerous work). They were men of daring, and you can see a bit of this romance in the later American fiction of the Doc Savage novels by Lester Dent.

Doyle continues to switch up his formula, even if he's using techniques he's mastered in previous stories. Although much of "The Engineer's Thumb" is a secondary character's testimony acting as a framing device, it's just as entertaining to read as it was in previous stories like *The Sign of the Four*. We see yet another reference to Inspector Bradstreet, which makes me think that Doyle was positioning him to be Holmes' Scotland Yard contact in the after-marriage phase of the partnership between Holmes and Watson, even though Lestrade has become the character we most associate in that role.

There are evil Germans (yes, even in the 1890s) and fiendish counterfeiters, but Holmes doesn't actually do much, and the criminals are never found — another one of Holmes' rare defeats (although these "rare defeats" seem to happen more often in *Adventures*). There are also internal inconsistencies, such as why the house is still burning hours later or how Hatherley manages to not bleed to death while unconscious, but it's still a fun, middle-of-the-range story.

The Adventure of the Noble Bachelor (1892)

In this adventure, Holmes is involved with another member of the nobility — this time, one from England. Surprisingly, Holmes is quite dismissive of the attention of the aristocracy:

"This looks like one of those unwelcome social summonses which call upon a man either to be bored or to lie."

Perhaps, though, it's somewhat understandable why Holmes might be bored with the aristocracy at this point. When researching Lord St. Simon, Holmes finds out that he was born in 1846 and that he is forty-one years of age. This dates the case either in 1887 or 1888, and thus at least several years after the start of Holmes' career as a consulting detective. However, we also learn that it's a few weeks before Watson's marriage, so it's after

The Sign of the Four and before "A Scandal in Bohemia." There's also a reference to another apocryphal case involving the son of the king of Scandinavia (as well as "the little problem of the Grosvenor Square furniture van"). It certainly seems that Holmes is flush with cases involving the nobility during this phase of his career, even if he hasn't yet received his most notorious one from the King of Bohemia, and a mere Lord may be dull by comparison.

While Holmes has refrained from lobbing sarcastic insults in previous cases, it's positively overflowing in this story. First, he takes a swipe at Lestrade when he's talking to Lord St. Simon:

"...That is what Mr. Lestrade, of Scotland Yard, looks upon as so serious. It is thought that Flora decoyed my wife out and laid some terrible trap for her."

"Well, it is a possible supposition."

"You think so, too?"

"I did not say a probable one..."

And again, at Lord St. Simon himself:

Lord St. Simon shook his head. "I am afraid that it will take wiser heads than yours or mine," he remarked, and bowing in a stately, old-fashioned manner he departed.

"It is very good of Lord St. Simon to honor my head by putting it on a level with his own," said Sherlock Holmes, laughing.

Later on, we get another look at Holmes' opinion of the British nobility, as he mentions his like of Americans:

"It is always a joy to meet an American, Mr. Moulton, for I am one of those who believe that the folly of a monarch and the blundering of a minister in far-gone years will not prevent our children from being some day citizens of the same world-wide country under a flag which shall be a quartering of the Union Jack with the Stars and Stripes."

Watson's broader knowledge (specifically his knowledge of high society) is useful to Holmes, providing another balance to Holmes' own body of knowledge. As a note, it was actually quite common at the time for younger members of the aristocracy to marry American heiresses. This is why the event isn't remarked on throughout the story — Doyle's audience would have been unsurprised by the arrangement, even if it might seem a little odd to us now.

It also appears that Doyle has become aware of the contradiction between Watson being injured in his shoulder and his leg, as the reference to his wound is simply in "one of my limbs." The page returns! Plus, there are a couple of references to Lord Backwater, who will appear in a later story.

The Adventure of the Beryl Coronet (1892)

Here we have another story about a jewel theft, and the story launches right into things. Doyle is becoming increasingly comfortable with focusing on only the details that matter in the stories, which is more of a modern literary technique than a Victorian one.

In this story, you see the use of a plot device which would later be called a "McGuffin" — i.e., something that drives the characters involved to extremes, and therefore acts to drive the plot. (A classic example of a McGuffin is the Maltese Falcon in the movie and novel of the same name.) While an object that motivates the characters in the story is hardly new (indeed, that's the central formula in most jewel heist stories, established in Wilkie Collins' highly-successful novel *The Moonstone* 24 years previously), what likens it to the later McGuffin concept is that the nature of the central object isn't explored all that thoroughly. In this case, we are told that the Beryl Coronet is owned by someone who is "a name which is a household word all over the earth — one of the highest, noblest, most exalted names in England," and that it's "[o]ne of the most precious public possessions of the empire," but that's about it. But it doesn't really matter, because the story isn't really about the coronet — it's about the people around it and what they do to each other to get it. In that respect, this is one of the most "noir" stories in the Holmes canon.

As for timing, the story appears to predate *The Sign of the Four* only because Watson says that he is looking out of "our bow-window" in Baker Street. In later stories, you may notice that Doyle is putting in less specific details, possibly in order to avoid introducing new continuity errors (and yet, Holmes shows that he doesn't have the strength to bend a golden coronet, even though in "The Speckled Band" he was able to unbend an iron poker, so it's not a perfect system). On the other hand, the last story in the book is believed to be the first time that Doyle decided that he was done with writing Sherlock Holmes, so it may have been more a case of writer fatigue than any interest in continuity.

The Adventure of the Copper Beeches (1892)

Some of the most interesting stuff in "The Copper Beeches" happens before the case even begins. It opens with another exploration of Holmes and Watson's relationship, as they argue about sensationalism and how it relates to Holmes' cases. Holmes congratulates Watson on focusing not on sensational trials or popular cases, but rather the smaller ones in which deduction and logical synthesis are showcased — or, more accurately, in which Holmes' powers are showcased. Watson can't help poking Holmes a bit, noting that he isn't completely absolved of being sensationalist, and reflects on Holmes' egotism and how it frustrates him. Holmes doubles down, defending his egotism by being more egotistical:

"If I claim full justice for my art, it is because it is an impersonal thing—a thing beyond myself. Crime is common. Logic is rare. Therefore it is upon the logic rather than upon the crime that you should dwell."

He then goes on to chastise not only Watson, but the general public and the criminal class as a whole for their lack of ingenuity.

This is one of the reasons why our fascination with the relationship between Holmes and Watson has endured over the years: because it feels very real. These two men are the best of friends, but they still have moments in which they get on each other's nerves and frustrate one another. They have fights and personal squabbles, and Doyle puts one right at the front of this story, correctly anticipating that the audience would find this an engaging part of the story, rather than a distraction from the mystery. At this point, we're starting to see that Doyle realizes his readers are just as interested in insights into Holmes and Watson as they are in the details of the extraordinary cases Holmes is involved in.

An interesting element in this opening scene is when Watson notices Holmes "answering, as was his wont, my thoughts rather than my words," something that Holmes disparaged as a "trick" back in *A Study in Scarlet* when it was done by C. Auguste Dupin. Thus do we see Watson's frustration with Holmes' egotism validated.

As for the timing of this case, it appears at first to be before Watson's marriage, but during the course of the story there are references to "A Scandal in Bohemia," "A Case of Identity," "The Man with the Twisted Lip," "The Noble Bachelor," and "The Blue Carbuncle." However, there isn't a single reference to Watson's wife. What does this say about Watson's married life by this point?

Another one of my favorite Holmes sayings is in this story:

"Data! data! data!" he cried impatiently. "I can't make bricks without clay."

During the case itself, Holmes makes a deduction about how the disposition of children can reflect the disposition of the parents, even though formal scientific study of developmental psychology didn't start until the early 20th century. Again, Doyle's medical background and his own keen sense of observation lend a level of scientific authenticity to his stories even before there was a rigorous understanding of such concepts.

Another interesting structural note is that we actually learn the answer to the mystery long before the end —

confirmation of the answer and some of the details of the story are left for the denouement.

Why I'm So Hard on Doyle at Times

With "The Copper Beeches," we come to the end of *The Adventures of Sherlock Holmes*, and the first third of the canon. I've heard that this was the first time that Doyle grew tired of writing for Holmes, but since *Memoirs* was released only a couple of years later, I don't know if that's the case. Regardless, it's a good point to pause and reflect on the past essays.

I've been pretty hard on Doyle thus far, particularly on his continuity. Part of the reason for this because I am an obsessive fanboy, and like all obsessive fanboys, I get frustrated by every mar and blemish, every missed detail, anything that might break me out of the conceit that this is all one universe. Some readers over the years have pointed out that people muddle and mix up details when they write down events well after the fact — therefore it is plausible that Watson would do so as well, and thus the inconsistencies aren't actually immersion-breaking. I tend to believe that people generally wouldn't forget things like where they've been wounded or when they were married, so I'm in the "no, they're really errors" camp.

I've also criticized Doyle's earlier writing techniques. I think that's important, because even during the course of *Adventures* you can see his writing style evolve and grow into the much more confident and masterful storyteller he's remembered as. Every writer evolves and changes, and turning a blind eye to the earlier missteps downplays the level of quality a writer attains in later life.

Whether it's his continuity or his style, though, I'm hard on Doyle because I love every aspect of his work. I enjoy picking apart the problems and examining them under a microscope just as much as I love watching two close friends bicker and reason their way to unraveling a mysterious case. I relish sitting down and critically analyzing these stories as much as I enjoy rereading them for pure enjoyment for the trillionth time. Each hits a different part of my brain, but it's all part of my love of Doyle and his characters.

So don't interpret my harsh remarks as hatred. Even the flawed stories like *A Study in Scarlet* I have read more times than other books I thoroughly adore. I do it because I love every brilliant, wonderful, irritating, misplaced word of the canon.

Plus, dead people are less likely to sue you when you say bad things about them.

The Memoirs of Sherlock Holmes

Silver Blaze (1892)

"Silver Blaze" is one of the most well-known stories in *The Memoirs of Sherlock Holmes*, primarily due to the famous line about "the curious incident of the dog":

> *"Is there any point to which you would wish to draw my attention?"*

> *"To the curious incident of the dog in the night-time."*

> *"The dog did nothing in the night-time."*

> *"That was the curious incident," remarked Sherlock Holmes.*

In fact, this quote is so popular that people often assume it actually shows up in completely different stories instead of this one — usually *The Hound of the Baskervilles* (another story involving dogs on the moors, but in a very different way).

For all the popularity of this quote, the story isn't the best representation of Holmes' skill. To start, Holmes doesn't dramatically uncover new evidence so much as sift through a large amount of existing evidence to draw the correct conclusion. Further, Holmes is uncharacteristically lucky in this case. He makes a number of guesses, and even he admits to being surprised when he is proven correct.

Many of these unusual quirks relate to "The Silver Blaze" being one of the few "fair play" mysteries in the canon. Fair play mysteries are when all the facts and characters are available to the reader as well as to the detective — something that's very common in mysteries today, but fairly infrequent in the stories of Doyle's time. It's harder to dramatically pull out the key piece of evidence when you also have to give the reader the same chance to discover it as well.

This is not the first time that horse racing has come up in the canon. Betting on horse races was a part of "Blue Carbuncle," and the allusion to Holmes' knowledge of horse betting in that story is reinforced when he places a bet himself in this one. Further, there is some question as to whether Holmes' bet was entirely ethical, as he bet on Silver Blaze when he clearly had inside information on the horse. It could be a case of Holmes being a bit naive about betting etiquette, but "Blue Carbuncle" seems to contradict that. Regardless, we learn that Holmes (and, in later stories, Watson) gambles, both with his money and with some of his deductions.

We also meet a new Scotland Yard inspector and one of the most talented, Inspector Gregory. Holmes considers Gregory to be an "extremely competent officer," lacking only in imagination. Gregory does prove to be quite clever, as well as diligent about preserving evidence. Gregory is also very respectful of Holmes' methods. As for the chronology of this case, Holmes and Watson are talking over breakfast at the start of the story in 221B which implies pre-marriage, since it's more likely that they would be having dinner or supper if Watson was visiting. However, there's a reference to Watson's published memoirs, and we learn that Holmes has come to earn the respect of at least one Scotland Yard detective, so it's probable that this is a late case in the pre-marriage period.

Holmes is uncommonly modest in this story. Not only does he admit to guessing, but he also admits to making a mistake in his deductions:

> "*Because I made a blunder, my dear Watson — which is, I am afraid, a more common occurrence than any one would think who only knew me through your memoirs.*"

Some more threads that we've been watching pop up in this story:

- This is another one of the few appearances of the "ear-flapped traveling-cap" — only the second in four books.
- There's a background reference to gypsies, similar to the one in "The Speckled Band."
- There's another example of Holmes' sense of personal justice: "I follow my own methods, and tell as much or as little as I choose."
- Watson again makes some good observations. He strikes upon a key point in the evidence (the stable-boy locking the door) and he notices the return tracks of the horse and man, saving them valuable time.

One of the better stories in the canon, and well worth reading.

A Quick Note: The Problem with "The Cardboard Box"

In many of the British editions of *The Memoirs of Sherlock Holmes*, the next story is "The Cardboard Box," but in American editions that story shows up in one of the later collections due to its being censored from *Memoirs*. For my reread when I was writing this book, I used ebooks that were based off of an American printing, so that's the story order I'm using. I'll be dealing with "The Cardboard Box" later on, but if you're using the British publication order, you should be able to jump ahead to that essay and then come back.

Why did I use the American versions? Because I already owned printed copies of the British versions, and I wanted to compare and contrast the two, so I used e-books based on the American publications. It was easier to use them as the roadmap while working on these essays, so a bias for the American versions has persisted as I make my way through. Some Sherlockians have expressed a preference for one version or the other, but for casual readers, the differences are relatively minor — just find a version of the canon and start reading.

The Adventure of the Yellow Face (1893)

"The Yellow Face" is an unusual story in the canon for two different reasons. The most noticeable one is that it details one of Holmes' failures (which, although Holmes has been no stranger to failure in the previous collection of short stories, is still a pretty rare occurrence). Although the truth of the situation does eventually come out, Holmes is quite wrong about the nature of the mysterious person in this story. Holmes is surprisingly modest about his failure at the very end of the story:

"Watson," said he, "if it should ever strike you that I am getting a little over-confident in my powers, or giving less pains to a case than it deserves, kindly whisper 'Norbury' in my ear, and I shall be infinitely obliged to you."

(By the way, Watson never does this in the canon, although a couple of pastiches have made use of this.)

The second and more surprising reason is that this story not only addresses interracial marriage in Victorian London, but it does so sympathetically. Granted, it was not illegal in England to have a child of mixed race (unlike in other countries at the time), but it was certainly considered to be shameful. Mrs. Munro claims she "cut myself off from [her] race" in marrying a black man — Sherlockian H. W. Bell points out that Georgia's laws at the time did prohibit such marriages, even if England did not — but Doyle doesn't hold back from painting the situation as anything but loving and accepting. In fact, this story is one of the more sentimental stories in the canon. This is tolerant for the 20th century, let alone the 19th.

To change focus to Doyle himself for a bit, this liberal attitude isn't entirely surprising. He was known for political campaigning and taking on seemingly hopeless causes. At the turn of the 20th century, he wrote a couple of pieces about the UK's role in the Boer War, and volunteered to work as a doctor during the conflict. He ran for office twice (but failed both times). He worked to reform the Congo Free State, and wrote passionately about the horrors going on there. He also personally investigated at least two criminal cases, and managed to get both men (George Edalji and Oscar Slater) exonerated as a result. Doyle was a man of strong convictions, and those convictions come out in this story, and in the character of Holmes and Watson (albeit in different ways).

Switching back to canon watching, there's another great scene of physical object deduction. It's on par with "The Blue Carbuncle," although it doesn't really relate to the case at hand. This time, Watson isn't in awe of the deduction, but instead tries to reconstruct Holmes' work, to limited success. Some of

Watson's writing starts to show his own budding deduction ability:

"From every gesture and expression I could see that he was a reserved, self-contained man, with a dash of pride in his nature, more likely to hide his wounds than to expose them."

In fact, Watson is actually comfortable criticizing Holmes' theory:

"What do you think of my theory?"

"It is all surmise."

On the other hand, Watson is more of an apologist for Holmes' drug use in this story than he was in earlier stories:

Save for the occasional use of cocaine, he had no vices, and he only turned to the drug as a protest against the monotony of existence when cases were scanty and the papers uninteresting.

Something worth noting at this point is that there are a number of editorial changes between the British and American editions of the canon beyond simply reordering the stories. This editorial license is most problematic in this story, because the American version of the story never actually mentions the child having a yellow face, which seems to contradict the title. However, a look over the British edition shows that the sentence "It was of a livid chalky white" originally read "It was of a livid dead yellow."

More bits of canon watching:

- There's another bit of backwards continuity, as there's a reference to the upcoming story "The Musgrave Ritual."

This is another American/British edition edit: in the original British edition it's a reference to "The Second Stain," but either way they are references to stories yet to be published.

- There's also another nod to Holmes' boxing skill: "Few men were capable of greater muscular effort, and he was undoubtedly one of the finest boxers of his weight that I have ever seen...." Doyle was quite the fan of boxing, and he even wrote a Gothic mystery about the sport in 1896 called *Rodney Stone*.
- The page not only makes another appearance, but he speaks!
- Another example of Holmes' disregard for the law: "Of course, legally, we are putting ourselves hopelessly in the wrong; but I think that it is worth it."

"The Yellow Face" is a wonderful story, and probably one of my favorites.

The Adventure of the Stock-Broker's Clerk (1893)

We find another confidence game in this story, similar to the one in "The Red-Headed League." Even the core ploy is similar: Mr. Hall Pycroft is given a false job in order to keep him out of the way for nefarious reasons. There's a strangely 21st century tone to the story, as the case revolves around identity theft, and I'm surprised that the various modern forms of Sherlock Holmes haven't adapted it yet. It's not a bad story, but the similarities to "The Red-Headed League" end up making this one of the more unremarkable mysteries, even though it gives us some interesting glimpses into Watson's life.

(As a side note, one of the criminals in this story is a "cracksman" or burglar. Doyle's brother-in-law, E. W. Hornung, wrote a series of stories about a gentleman cracksman named A. J. Raffles. If you're interested, the first one is called *The Amateur Cracksman*. It's also in the public domain, so you should be able to find an e-book version for free or cheap.)

The timing of the story appears to be a few months after *The Sign of the Four*, since Watson has just settled into married life and Holmes asks about Mrs. Watson's recovery from the events of that novel. We learn a bit more about Watson's home life as a married man, as well as his medical practice (which he purchased from a retiring doctor). We learn that he reads the *British Medical Journal*, so he keeps up-to-date on medical practices. It seems that married life agreed with Watson at some point, because here he mentions that he "had confidence…in my youth and energy," when in *A Study in Scarlet* he confessed that he was extremely lazy!

It's also telling that Holmes is calling on Watson at his home so soon after their marriage, which shows how much Holmes values his partner's presence on certain cases. It's not surprising that he values Watson, given that trying to untangle the chronology of previous stories has shown that they lived together for years before Watson got married, but Holmes has admitted that he has difficulty making friends, so it seems he would rather try to keep the one he has managed to make rather than going through the futile efforts of finding new friends.

By the end of the story, Holmes doesn't really solve the case — he just happens to be in the right place at the right time. Even the key piece of information about the robbery is conveniently provided by the thief's brother! Granted, Holmes did manage to help the police to capture the partner for the robbery, but he didn't crack the case wide open by any stretch of the imagination. Given Holmes' lackluster involvement in the case and the strong similarities to the plot of a previous case, this ends up being one of the weaker stories.

The Adventure of the 'Gloria Scott' (1893)

"Gloria Scott" is the first case Holmes was ever involved with, so let's dig a little deeper into this one. There are a few similarities, both fortunate and unfortunate, between this story and *A Study in Scarlet*. Both stories feature iconic moments in the history of Sherlock Holmes — in this case, acting very much as an origin story for the Great Detective. Unfortunately, "Gloria Scott" shares the flaw of being only half a Sherlock Holmes story, as the second half is entirely taken up with a narrative that explains the events behind the case. And both stories introduce snarls in chronology that make it hard to work the other cases around.

The confession that Trevor left indicates that the events on the Gloria Scott happened in 1855. Later, he writes that "For more than twenty years we have led peaceful and useful lives," which would put the story at 1875 at the earliest, which is consistent with Holmes being in college, and makes the idea that *A Study in Scarlet* takes place around the early 1880s plausible. However, when Hudson meets Trevor, he says "'Why, it's thirty year and more since I saw you last....'," which would make the events of the story 1885, and pretty much impossible to reconcile with the established canon. I choose to think that Hudson is a liar, and I stick with the 1875 date, but the problems go much deeper than this — "Gloria Scott" is probably the epitome of chronology snarling.

Holmes mentions that he was in college for only two years, and that he was schooled in fencing and boxing. He confirms that he wasn't "a very sociable fellow," and that he only had one friend at school — and said friend ends up taking a somewhat similar role as Watson did in Holmes' early cases. Surprisingly, Holmes also notes that he originally didn't consider being a detective, but that his deductive skills were merely a hobby:

"One evening, shortly after my arrival, we were sitting over a glass of port after dinner, when young Trevor began to talk about those habits of observation and inference which I had already formed into a system, although I had not yet appreciated the part which they were to play in my life."

And later:

"'I don't know how you manage this, Mr. Holmes, but it seems to me that all the detectives of fact and of fancy would be children in your hands. That's your line of life, sir, and you may take the word of a man who has seen something of the world.'

"And that recommendation, with the exaggerated estimate of my ability with which he prefaced it, was, if you will believe me, Watson, the very first thing which ever made me feel that a profession might be made out of what had up to that time been the merest hobby."

Despite the similarities to the structure in *Scarlet*, this is still quite a departure from the Holmes formula. Not only is it the first case that doesn't feature Watson in any meaningful way, but it's the first case told from Holmes' perspective. Granted, Holmes doesn't do a lot of deduction during the case, but we do see glimpses of him explaining his thought process, especially when he decodes the cypher. And the story in Trevor's confession is interesting in and of itself. It is even pointed to by scholars as the likely origin of the phrase "smoking gun" as meaning a damning piece of evidence:

> "...there he lay with his brains smeared over the chart of the Atlantic which was pinned upon the table, while the chaplain stood with a smoking pistol in his hand at his elbow."

But despite an interesting attempt to do something new in a Holmes story, it ends up being mediocre. I'm not as frustrated by this story as I am with *Scarlet* (at least we know who all the narrators are this time!), but the glimpse into Holmes' past ends up being too short and too consumed by the drama of the Gloria Scott, which ultimately ends with both threads being only somewhat resolved.

The Adventure of the Musgrave Ritual (1893)

Right after "Gloria Scott," we have another case in Holmes' pre-Watson career — his fourth, assuming we count "Gloria Scott" as his first, and it was neither of the cases he undertook when he had rooms at Montague Street. This one has far more flair and character than "Gloria Scott." Here we have more exploration of Holmes' early adult life, a good old-fashioned treasure hunt, some intrigue and romance, and the introduction of more staples of the Holmes canon. In fact, this story is so iconic that the Baker Street Irregulars recite the ritual itself during their annual dinner, and T. S. Eliot paraphrased the ritual in his play *Murder in the Cathedral*. This story is listed as one of Doyle's favorites, and on reflection, it's probably one of mine as well — a great, classic read.

Like the previous story, this one doesn't feature Watson in a support role and has Holmes as the primary narrator. As such, we get another glimpse in Holmes' methods from his own words:

"You know my methods in such cases, Watson. I put myself in the man's place and, having first gauged his intelligence, I try to imagine how I should myself have proceeded under the same circumstances."

Holmes mentions more apocryphal cases (and failures), as well as some of the details of his college days. This leads to another interesting question of canon lore: what college did Holmes go to? Even though three stories now reference Holmes' college days, none of them specify which college it was, although many Sherlockians (including the highly influential Sherlockian William Baring-Gould) have narrowed the debate to being between Oxford and Cambridge. Personally, I'm inclined against Cambridge, as he doesn't seem to recognize or remark on anything when his cases take him to the Cambridge area, but I've seen evidence both ways.

One of the things he may have studied was phrenology, the (now debunked) science of studying the measurements of the human head to determine behavioral characteristics. For example, in "The Blue Carbuncle," Holmes mentions the size of the skull as an indication of intelligence. But his interest was not unusual — many in Victorian England believed in phrenology. During "The Musgrave Ritual," Reginald Musgrave described his intelligent butler, Brunton:

"'He was a well-grown, handsome man, with a splendid forehead....'"

In fact, Brunton is a quietly unrecognized contribution to literature. This is one of the stories in which the cliché of "the butler did it" originated, but it also plays to a second trope, that of the intelligent servant who outwits their employer (best seen in P. G. Wodehouse's "Jeeves" stories and novels). However, while this case is probably the first detective story in which the butler is the culprit, there are actually surprisingly few mystery stories overall in which one of the servants is responsible for the crime. Many use the butler as a red herring, subverting the cliché early on in the 20th century, even though it persists to this day. The reason why these tropes were so strong at the time was due to the utter reliance that the upper and middle class had on their servants, and the notion that they might somehow be untrustworthy was terrifying. You can compare it our growing reliance on technology, and the subsequent rise in movies and stories that feature robots, machines, and other technology turning or being turned against humanity.

Aside from the contributions to Holmes' past and to literature in general, this story has a few nuggets of information about the Baker Street years (which is the frame for this story). Watson talks about Holmes' slovenly habits again, but this time contrasts it with Holmes' extreme neatness of dress. Watson admits to being a bit of a slob himself, but not as much as Holmes. In Watson's description of (and frustration with) Holmes' habits, we get some of the most iconic images of their rooms at Baker Street (punctuated with a dry sense of humor which is, overall, extremely subtle in the canon):

But with me there is a limit, and when I find a man who keeps his cigars in the coal-scuttle, his tobacco in the toe end of a Persian slipper, and his unanswered correspondence transfixed by a jack-knife into the very center of his wooden mantelpiece, then I begin to give myself virtuous airs. I have always held, too, that pistol practice should be distinctly an open-air pastime; and when Holmes, in one of his queer humors, would sit in an arm-chair with his hair-trigger and a hundred Boxer cartridges, and proceed to adorn the opposite wall with a patriotic V. R. done in bullet-pocks, I felt strongly that neither the atmosphere nor the appearance of our room was improved by it.

The Adventure of the Reigate Squires (1893)

First, a bit of clarity about the title. This story was originally published as "The Reigate Squire," but was subsequently renamed as "The Reigate Squires" when collected into *Memoirs*. When it was published in America in Harper's Weekly, it was changed to "The Reigate Puzzle," and subsequent reprintings of the American *Memoirs* retain the American title. I'm more familiar with the story under "Squires" rather than "Puzzle," so that's what I'll defer to, even though I'm using the American version for reference.

Prior to this story, we've had references to various apocryphal cases, but this is the first time in which the consequences of an undocumented case impacts a documented one — in this instance, Holmes becoming ill. I consider this to be the turning point in the apocrypha of the Holmes canon. Thus far, the references have been scattered here and there, teasing indications of the life of Holmes outside of what we read. But with "The Reigate Squires," I really feel that the world of Holmes and Watson comes alive. The various ways Doyle makes Holmes and Watson seem like a part of the world have, in this story, gelled into a cohesive world of its own. Whether it reflects or ties into the contemporary world of Doyle's original audience, this story makes the narrative reality of Holmes and Watson feel less like a jumble of facts and dates and more like an organic reality that I want to know more about and be a part of. Even when I stop reading the stories, in some part of my mind Holmes and Watson still exist, solving crimes and thwarting villains that I will never see and know about. As this story turns the corner from me getting frustrated with the organic nature of the canon to embracing it, this is also one of the few stories that actually provide a firm date for creating timelines — April 14, 1887. (During the writing of this book, I realized that April 14th is also my wedding anniversary. I will never be able to convince anyone that the date is anything but a coincidence.)

Some of this feeling of emotional reality comes out as we learn more about how Watson cares for Holmes. We meet Colonel Hayter, who is a former patient of Watson's in Afghanistan. We find out that Watson cares deeply for Holmes, so much that he's willing to butt heads with Holmes and admonish him not to take any new cases while he is recovering from his illness. Of course, Watson ultimately loses the battle of wills, but his stubborn refusal to cave to Holmes' ego and pouting shows another side of Watson's support for his friend, and how he's willing to go against Holmes himself to do what is best. In the end it is the mental puzzle that causes Holmes to recuperate, showing that Watson cares for Holmes far more than he understands Holmes.

There are some interesting juxtapositions of Holmes' analytical skills with his showmanship. Twice Holmes uses his illness to make "mistakes" that progress the case, another indication of his acting skill. He also explicitly mentions his alleged transparency, mentioning that "it has always been my habit to hide none of my methods." He tosses out that he made "twenty-three other deductions" which he glosses over, making the assumption that his audience has no interest in the level of minutia they detail (or, as some more cynical Sherlockians have pointed out, he may have been lying just to make himself seem more impressive in his diminished state). It shows that Holmes is coming to terms with the necessity of combining his scientific methods with more popular interest in order to spread word of his methods and, naturally, his own career.

The Adventure of the Crooked Man (1893)

Although this is another interesting case of a romantic triangle and another example of a Sherlockian "locked room" mystery, this story is better recognized for showing a different side of the post-marriage Holmes and Watson relationship. It's been a long time (since "The Man with the Twisted Lip") since we've seen Watson's home, but for the second time, Holmes comes there to meet Watson.

This time, Holmes imposes himself on Watson's hospitality by arriving at a very late hour and making himself immediately at home. The fact that Watson doesn't seem particularly put out by this is telling about both the nature of their friendship and Watson's tolerance of Holmes' strange habits. During this scene, however, Holmes makes a series of rapid-fire deductions almost immediately upon entering the Watson home, but there isn't really a reason for him to do so. Whether it's to keep Watson disoriented or because Holmes knows that such deductions generally delight and amaze Watson, either way I think he does it to defuse Watson's frustration at the late hour in which Holmes imposes himself on his old friend. During the bombardment of deductions, though, Holmes teases Watson about "keeping him up," and even takes a shot at his chronicler at the lack of "playing fair" in the previously documented cases:

"The same may be said, my dear fellow, for the effect of some of these little sketches of yours, which is entirely meretricious, depending as it does upon your retaining in your own hands some factors in the problem which are never imparted to the reader."

The shot is probably Doyle expressing his frustration with writing the stories. There are only three more stories after this one until (spoiler alert!) he attempts to kill off Holmes, and his reluctance to continue writing the stories shows through in the exchange between Holmes and Watson. On the other hand, the conflict on whether or not Holmes has emotions — something that has come up time and again in previous stories — takes another turn. By degrees, Doyle has tried to reshape Holmes' apparent emotionlessness into something that exists more on the surface instead of Holmes having an extreme of being either utterly emotional or utterly emotionless. He brings up this new approach on two separate occasions in this story to drive home the point:

His eyes kindled and a slight flush sprang into his thin cheeks. For an instant only. When I glanced again his face had resumed that red-Indian composure which had made so many regard him as a machine rather than a man.

and

In spite of his capacity for concealing his emotions, I could easily see that Holmes was in a state of suppressed excitement...

Ultimately, Holmes asks for Watson's help on the case, but Watson doesn't really contribute much. Sadly, this is the start of a slow slide from a sharp and talented Watson assisting a brilliant but flawed Holmes to Watson being just a chronicler to Holmes' unerring genius.

There's a brief mention of Holmes' "Baker Street Boys," the street urchins that work for him, although instead of Wiggins, we meet a new one: Simpson. (Sadly, this is also the last time we hear mention of the Irregulars in the canon, despite their well-entrenched status in the Holmes myth.) Holmes also displays his knowledge of the Bible, even though Watson ranked Holmes' knowledge of literature and philosophy to be "nil" in *A Study in Scarlet*.

Finally, while I've already ranted about the complete omission of the phrase "Elementary, my dear Watson" in the canon, this story contains an exchange that is probably the closest to it:

> *"I have the advantage of knowing your habits, my dear Watson," said he....*

> *"Excellent!" I cried.*

> *"Elementary," said he.*

The Adventure of the Resident Patient (1893)

More edition wackiness here. Remember how I said that in American printings of *Memoirs* the story "The Cardboard Box" was removed? Well, they thought the opening scene for the story was so impressive that they cut it out and stuck it at the front of this story. However, when "The Cardboard Box" makes its eventual appearance in the American printing of *His Last Bow*, the scene is there as well! In the interest of not repeating myself, I'm going to skip my commentary on that scene, which consists of a series of amazing deductions by Holmes as well as a case of his outright hypocrisy. If you're interested in that, jump ahead to my comments on "The Cardboard Box."

But in either version of the story, we see another instance of Doyle becoming disenchanted with writing stories about his detective, right off the bat:

Glancing over the somewhat incoherent series of Memoirs with which I have endeavored to illustrate a few of the mental peculiarities of my friend Mr. Sherlock Holmes....

He even takes a mild swipe at *A Study in Scarlet* and "Gloria Scott" on the way out of the first paragraph, but that paragraph adds another piece of the continuity puzzle — at least, one version of it does. In the original Strand version of the text (not the American version that contains the hastily added scene from "The Cardboard Box"), Watson says that it must have taken place "towards the end of the first year" in which he and Holmes take rooms on Baker Street. The reference to the 'Gloria Scott,' however, indicates that Holmes must have told Watson that story before this one, so he must have related that story to Watson fairly early on in their relationship. While it doesn't settle much in terms of questions of case continuity, it does show that Holmes opened up to Watson somewhere around several *months* into their relationship, instead of the implied answer of several *years* — an interesting indication on how quickly Holmes started trusting and confiding in his lone friend.

After the last story, Doyle swings Watson back to his earlier mode of being intelligent, explaining that Watson was "sufficiently conversant with Holmes' methods to be able to follow his reasoning" and reverse-engineer one of his deductions. This happening so early in their relationship does seem to contradict some of Watson's amazement at Holmes' methods in the previous cases, however. This disconnect has led to a certain amount of Watson apologism, claiming that Watson was actually never stupid, but rather too modest. This camp maintains that Watson likely altered the recordings of his cases to reduce his own deductions and intellect in order to bolster the skills and aptitudes of his friend. They point to sections such as in "The Blue Carbuncle" where Watson modestly underrates his own abilities, and this camp maintains that his inadequacy comes not from his intellect, but from his editing skill in being unable to excise more remnants of his own talent. Obviously this line of thinking ties in well to The Great Game, but some non-Game-playing Sherlockians have posited this as well.

Being a Watson fan, I want to believe this line of logic, but the idea causes my head to explode when I consider it at any depth. For this to work, you have to assume that Watson is an unreliable narrator. We get all our information about Watson and Holmes from Watson (with the exception of three stories in the later canon), so if we assume that Watson is an unreliable narrator, anything he tells us about himself or his friend is suspect. This actually addresses some lingering issues like inconsistencies in chronology and the back and forth waffling on whether Holmes has emotions or not. But if an author uses an unreliable narrator, he does it with some purpose in mind, and I don't see that purpose when I review the supposedly unreliable sections of the canon.

I've heard the theory that Doyle might have come to realize that he had made some errors and started to intentionally make Watson unreliable in order to explain away those problems, but that doesn't seem consistent with his growing boredom with the characters — why would he go through the trouble of making his narrator unreliable when he's going to kill off Holmes in a few stories anyway? I mean, he even recycles the ending for "The Five Orange Pips" in this story — once again, the villains escape and then are mysteriously killed at sea. How can Doyle be simultaneously so careless and so nuanced in his writing? While it is technically possible for Doyle to be thinking and creating his stories on these levels, the more likely answer is that Doyle cranked out these stories as inspiration (and money) motivated him, and he just wasn't paying that much attention to the little details. Ergo, moving Watson more and more to an observing role and Holmes taking up the lion's share of deduction is easier and less taxing than writing two flawed but complex characters. Every writer has off days, and every writer has some stories come out better than others.

So in the end, while the Watson fan in me really wants to believe that this is all part of Doyle's plan to use Watson's unreliability as a method to underrate his own intelligence and talent, it just doesn't add up. Watson's talent shows through in spite of Doyle's intentions, not because of them.

Anyhow, the case itself is another con game with bits of "The Five Orange Pips" worked in. We meet an Inspector Lanner, but we barely see him in this story and never see him again in the course of the canon, so forget about him. Most of the interesting bits of the story actually belong to "The Cardboard Box" anyhow. It's not a bad story for all that, but it looks particularly weak next to upcoming stories like "The Greek Interpreter" and "The Final Problem."

The Adventure of the Greek Interpreter (1893)

This story is most noteworthy for being the story in which we learn more about Sherlock's family, and especially the introduction of Sherlock's brother, Mycroft Holmes. (For clarity, I will always refer to Mycroft by his first name. Thus, if I refer to "Holmes" at any point, I'm talking about Sherlock, not Mycroft.)

Aside from his brother, we learn that Sherlock's ancestors were country squires, and that his grandmother was the sister of the French artist Vernet. There are actually several French painters with the last name of Vernet, but Emile Jean Horace Vernet seems to have lived at the right time, so I assume it's him. While the story of Sherlock's family ends there, some research on Horace Vernet shows that he was primarily a painter of battles and portraits in a very accurate, detailed style, rather than the idealized style that was common at the time. While Sherlock claims that "Art in the blood is liable to take the strangest forms," the Holmes family may have inherited that combination of artistic flair and attention to detail that perfectly describes both brothers. I'm inclined to think that this was an intentional choice by Doyle, if only because it so neatly explains the growing conflict in Sherlock's character: that bizarre marriage between his love of the purely analytical and the flair for the dramatic.

By Sherlock's own words, Mycroft has more intellect but less energy. Mycroft is the elder and more intelligent brother, but is disinclined to put in the work to confirm his own theories. While Sherlock chides Mycroft's lassitude, in many stories we've seen Sherlock lying in a stupor when a case isn't engaging him — an echo of his older brother. It's also telling that Sherlock faults

Mycroft's lack of interest in acquiring enough evidence for the British legal system, when in multiple stories he himself has destroyed evidence or let criminals go to suit his own sense of justice. But the parallels go both ways: as Mycroft speaks with Sherlock and Watson, he pulls out a snuff box, showing that both Holmes brothers are casual drug users. And, of course, both brothers are able to casually insult the other without raising much ire (which, in Sherlock's case, seems to be a very rare thing).

It is impossible to talk about Mycroft without talking about the Diogenes Club, that strange establishment in which men go to be social while simultaneously remaining in absolute silence. Mycroft's and the club's connections to the British government are only hinted at in this story, but they come up again in future canonical references. The idea of the Diogenes Club has taken such a hold on later writers that it has not only shown up in other Sherlock Holmes pastiches, but also generated its own pastiches that don't even include any of the characters for the Holmes canon!

Before we meet Mycroft, though, Watson waffles somewhat in his previously warm perception of Sherlock's emotional state:

[S]ometimes I found myself regarding him as an isolated phenomenon, a brain without a heart, as deficient in human sympathy as he was pre-eminent in intelligence.

It's possible that this could just be hyperbole, an attempt to paint a picture for the audience to contrast Sherlock before and after the revelation of his family. I'm inclined to believe this, as we do see Sherlock becoming far more emotional over the course of this story and the rest of the stories in this book.

Sherlock also mentions bringing Gregson in on the case, another indication that Sherlock considers him to be the most talented detective in Scotland Yard… not Lestrade.

Even though Sherlock himself makes for a rather poor showing here, both Mycroft and Watson really shine in this story — indeed, they do just about all of the work in the case! As such, this is a great story for background and information, but isn't one of the best stories in the canon for showcasing Sherlock's abilities.

The Adventure of the Naval Treaty (1893)

This story is another literary first — in this case, one of the very first stories in what we now consider to be the espionage genre. It is also the longest short story in the canon, and part of the final run of really good stories in the last third or so of *Memoirs*. While it doesn't have canon-defining elements like the earlier "Greek Interpreter" or the upcoming "Final Problem," there's still a lot to dig into with this story.

This story was released relatively close to the start of World War I. In that war, France and Russia were strong allies to England, but in this story, they are seen as potential enemies who might benefit from the theft of the treaty. This is accurate of the political climate of the time, though, showing the radical shift in politics that the First World War brought about (and proving that it's always fashionable to make the French and the Russians look like the bad guys).

Also, it's fascinating to note how nepotism is perceived here: Phelps isn't ashamed to note that he got his job as a government official because his uncle was a minister, a situation that would have caused a major political scandal if it had happened today. There's also a case of Holmes making a note of something on his shirt-cuff, but that's not all that uncommon at the time. In fact, Harry Furniss talked in "The Confessions of a Caricaturist" (1902) about doodling pictures on his shirt-cuff. It's something you did when you didn't have a piece of paper handy to make a note on — the modern equivalent would be writing a note on your hand or on the back of a receipt.

Another cultural aspect that avid readers of Victorian fiction will run into a lot is "brain fever." While there's some speculation as to what this ailment actually was (or even if it was only one ailment at all), it was a recognized medical complaint at the time. It also happened to be a useful literary device to make a character temporarily deranged and immobile for weeks or even months at a time, which is likely why it was very popular in novels — a more modern example of this would be the over-reliance of knocking people unconscious by hitting them on the head in crime fiction, or the prevalence of convenient amnesia in soap operas. One of the most well-known appearances of brain fever is in Emily Brontë's *Wuthering Heights*, but the concept extended to French literature as well, such as its appearance in Gustave Flaubert's *Madame Bovary*. Many believed that brain fever came from excessive stress or heartbreak, which is why it is commonly attributed to female characters, but this story shows that even men could fall victim to it.

Whether it was a real illness or not, it became a common trope (and cliché) of fiction of the day, and Doyle was certainly not immune to literary fads. In fact, he spoke about it in a speech on May 22, 1905 to the Royal Medical and Chirurgical Society of London:

"There is then that mysterious malady which is known as brain fever. What should we novelists do without that wonderful fever? What would she nurse him through during that anxious time, and how else could he, after many months of continual delirium, come to himself and proclaim himself a chastened and a better man?"

Speaking of narrative structure, this story feels almost American in composition to me. A lot of the American detective fiction in the early 20th century focused on getting information from people instead of examining physical evidence — the works of Dashiell Hammett and Raymond Chandler, for example, are replete with scenes of detectives interrogating suspects, instead of focusing on the examination of clues and collecting evidence. This story is similar, showing a lot more of Holmes trying to pick apart each person's testimony and construct a series of events over his usual methods of observation. This certainly wasn't an unusual format — the Max Carrados stories by Ernest Bramah, for example, tend to focus on dialog and interrogation — but this story is a more explicit example of that style of mystery-writing, and it provides an interesting contrast to the usual construction of a Holmes story.

Aside from the cultural aspects, there is some more exploration of the subtler parts of the canon worth noting here. It's easy to lose them between the introduction of Mycroft Holmes in the previous story and Professor Moriarty in the following one, but let's take some time to pull them out.

Using only the canon as a guide, dating this case is actually very straight-forward, but bringing in historic events makes the situation worse. This is a post-marriage case, and it is "the July that immediately succeeded" that event. However, there is a mention about a secret treaty between England and Italy which is, at the time of the case, just being discussed in the press. This was a real treaty, but historically it was drafted in 1887, not 1888. This gives more weight to the marriage being in 1887, unless you only use canonical cues. (Yes, we're closing in on halfway through the canon, and we still can't get any closure on what year the second novel was set in!) I'm still inclined to think that Doyle muddled what year the treaty was signed in and assumed it was closer to 1888 — after all, this story was published six years after those events, and I sometimes forget whether something happened in 2006 or 2007, so that's plausible to me.

Apocryphal cases pop up again in this story, such as "The Adventure of the Tired Captain." Interesting, there's a lengthy mention of "The Adventure of the Second Stain" here. "The Second Stain" is a canonical story, but it won't be written for another eleven years, so at the time this story was written it was an apocryphal case — an interesting example of Doyle going back to mine his own references for inspiration in later years.

Watson's past is fleshed out more with the introduction of his old school friend, Percy Phelps. Although Phelps is modest and tries to downplay his status, it says something about Watson's own status as a gentleman that he is able to become good friends with the nephew of a high-ranking government official. At this point in the canon, we've gotten hints and clues that both Watson and Holmes are so-called "men of good breeding," even if they start off their relationship quite poor financially. This is also the first time we actually learn that Watson has a mustache, but that he didn't have one while he was at school. We don't learn much more about Watson's mustache, but they were fashionable among military officers at the time, so I'm personally inclined to believe that Watson grew it during his time in the service, and the habit stayed with him after his retirement.

Holmes also gets some more development in this story, as Doyle continues to evolve his detective into a more emotional character. At one point, Holmes displays sudden reverence for a rose (although whether this was genuine or a sham is open to debate), and later Holmes admits that he "never can resist a touch of the dramatic." He also gets positively sulky when Watson even hints that he has to go back to his medical practice.

We also learn more about Holmes' relationship with the police, which he relates to the latest in the herd of Scotland Yard detectives, Mr. Forbes. He expressly admits that he has only taken credit in four of the last fifty-three cases he's worked with the police on, which may explain why Watson was motivated to chronicle some of Holmes' cases himself — out of a sense of injustice to the lack of credit his friend has received in the public eye. (Indeed, Holmes has repeatedly mentioned in previous stories that Watson's chronicles are much of the source of his fame, not through police reports in the newspapers.) It appears that Scotland Yard has far more respect for Holmes than he does for it, as he can get away with threatening a junior Yard detective without apparent repercussions.

We have the first instance (second if you count Mycroft) of someone not being impressed with Holmes' deductions, when Joseph Harrison says "For a moment I thought you had done something clever" after Holmes rattles off his usual series of insightful deductions upon meeting him. I'm inclined to believe this is another case of Doyle getting a bit bored with the character, or at least bored with writing the same scene of amazingly deducing information about a person over and over.

Some more points of our previously mentioned canon-watching:

- There's another appearance of the page. I really have no idea why I completely missed this character in all my previous reads. Sure, he's usually only in a sentence of two, but he's shown up about as much as Mrs. Hudson at this point.
- Speaking of Mrs. Hudson, she is mentioned here, and we learn that she isn't the most inventive cook, but she does do a good breakfast.
- This is another case that Watson brings to Holmes' attention (much like in "The Engineer's Thumb").
- There's another long night-time vigil, and Holmes even mentions the one in "The Speckled Band" as a similar experience.

Compared to the stories on both sides of it, "The Naval Treaty" is an often-missed gem in the canon, even if it's not one of the classics.

The Final Problem (1893)

Professor Moriarty

Now we come to this, the final story in the *Memoirs* and what Doyle believed would be the final Holmes story ever. Of course, we now know that Holmes survived his encounter and went on to appear in five more books. However, between the dramatic nature of the story's end and the fact that the next book (*The Hound of the Baskervilles*) wasn't published until eight years after this story, "The Final Problem" is commonly looked at as a natural end-point for the first part of the canon.

And what an end-point it is. There's not really a proper mystery in this story, but plenty of adventure. There are a lot of changes to the formula, and a number of intriguing references contained within. But most notably, this story is known for being the introduction of Holmes' more notorious foe, Professor James Moriarty (who has not yet gained a first name in this story, although his brother also goes by James). Since "The Final Problem" contains the most information about Holmes' nemesis, I'll spend most of my time discussing him here.

First off, it's interesting that Doyle introduces one of his most pivotal and iconic villains in the story in which he plans to kill Holmes off. But according to letters Doyle wrote at the time, his intention was to give Holmes an adversary that is worthy of his skill, so that Holmes' demise could be seen as a sacrifice, ridding the world of a notorious evil.

Moriarty is a fantastic example of a particular style of antagonist — the shadow or "evil twin" of the protagonist. Moriarty is similar to Holmes in many ways. Both men are scientists, who have applied logical reasoning to the matter of law (whether upholding it or violating it). Both men are incredibly observant. Both of them are capable of crafting elaborate plans and strategies that can span large areas and equally large lengths of time. Even Holmes admits the equality of the two, giving Moriarty his now legendary title of "the Napoleon of crime" and confessing a grudging respect for the man to Watson:

"...I had at last met an antagonist who was my intellectual equal. My horror at his crimes was lost in my admiration at his skill."

But the scene where Holmes and Moriarty meet is the best example of how the antagonist is the shadow of the protagonist.

> *" 'All that I have to say has already crossed your mind,'* said he.*

> *" 'Then possibly my answer has crossed yours,' I replied.*

> *" 'You stand fast?'*

> *" 'Absolutely.'*

Of course, such a confrontation between two scientific minds will involve some scientific theories. I've already mentioned the Victorian obsession with phrenology, and Moriarty's first words to Holmes are nothing short of a phrenological insult, saying that Holmes has "less frontal development" than expected. But in Holmes' description of Moriarty to Watson, we see something of the (now outdated) theory that criminal instincts are inherited.

> *"But the man had hereditary tendencies of the most diabolical kind. A criminal strain ran in his blood, which, instead of being modified, was increased and rendered infinitely more dangerous by his extraordinary mental powers."*

Although Holmes will only match wits with Moriarty in one more case, he is mentioned in five stories in total (which is about as many as Irene Adler), but this story is by far the most powerful and engaging exploration the character. While I look at some of the other minor characters in the canon and wonder how they became to ensnared in the greater mythology of Sherlock Holmes, there's no doubt in my mind why Moriarty has the place he does in the minds of Doyle's fans. Even if this glimpse in

Holmes' nemesis is tantalizingly brief, we fully believe that this is a villain that is utterly equal to Holmes' skill, and utterly worthy of defeat. He stands the test of time as one of the greatest villains in literature, and with good reason.

The Death of Sherlock Holmes

According to this story, Sherlock Holmes "died" on May 3rd, 1891. Doyle wanted to stop writing the series because he felt that it was distracting him from his more serious work, and he needed to be able to focus on his career outside of Sherlock Holmes. However, the public did not react so well to the story. The Strand's subscription numbers dropped by 200,000, and thousands of people wore black armbands in mourning. The public was furious. To give you a sense of this, imagine what would happen if J. K. Rowling suddenly killed Harry Potter off halfway through the series. But here we can see more of Doyle's frustrations, though the voice of Watson:

In an incoherent and, as I deeply feel, an entirely inadequate fashion, I have endeavored to give some account of my strange experiences in his company....

Let's look at the date of Holmes' fall and work it into our understanding of the continuity so far. 1891 means that Watson has been married for three or four years by the time Holmes goes to Reichenbach Falls. There is mention of the cooling of their friendship by 1890, but many of the post-marriage cases appear to take place relatively soon after Watson ties the knot, so that actually fits quite well together. If we consider that the two met sometime in the early 1880s, this means they were friends for less than a decade before Holmes "dies." It's not a very long time, but considering Holmes claims over a thousand cases that he's been involved with by this point, it's clearly been a very full ten years.

It's nice to see Doyle go back to his technique of providing a groundwork in reality for his stories. Watson mentions a few news articles and a specific letter as if they were well-known items of the day, even though they didn't exist at all. It's something he did a lot of in his earlier stories, and it's telling to compare stories like *A Study in Scarlet*, where this happened quite a bit, with many of the stories in *Memoirs* which usually only reference other canonical stories and apocryphal cases (although this story does plenty of that, especially to quickly build up Moriarty's reputation as a master criminal). But both tactics create the impression of a larger world, something that exists outside of the stories we read. Regardless of whether he's attempting to tie events to the real world of his readers or to the shared knowledge of his fictional stories, the point remains that each story feels like it exists in a space larger than itself. Nowadays, such continuity-building is common and even expected, but it really was quite a radical thing at the time, and even here in this supposedly final Holmes story, we see Doyle working to provide a broader context for his characters.

There are a few interesting touches on the previous stories scattered throughout. We again hear of Mycroft, soon after his initial appearance in "The Greek Interpreter," although he is acting in ways that seem like he is not nearly as lazy as Holmes led Watson to believe. Holmes dons another clever disguise, and shows his mastery of languages by speaking fluent Italian. Watson uses his friend's own methods of deduction to piece together Holmes' demise — a clever and touching tribute to Holmes that his friend finally mastered enough of his methods to help solve his murder (although we don't learn how much he gets right until Holmes' return in "The Empty House"). On the other hand, the famous rooms at Baker Street are set on fire, a touch that clearly communicates to the audience just how high the stakes are for Holmes and Watson.

We see a lot more of Holmes' tender feelings for Watson in this story. Although Holmes seems to be strangely invigorated and in light spirits while Moriarty is trying to kill him, he's very serious when it comes to putting Watson in the same danger. Twice Holmes tries to dissuade Watson for helping him — not because Holmes doesn't desire his friend's company, but rather because he is afraid that Watson will get hurt or killed by Moriarty's plans. Even when he confronts Moriarty at Reichenbach Falls, Holmes asks for (and gets) time to write some final words to reassure Watson. Although Holmes believes he is going to die, he still shows a final kindness to his one and only friend.

And thus concludes the first half of the Holmes canon, and the last story written in the 19th century. This is one of my favorite stories, as well as one of Doyle's. It has a well-deserved reputation as a pivotal story in the canon, and is certainly one of the ten best Holmes stories ever.

The Hound of the Baskervilles (1901-1902)

The Hound of the Baskervilles is my favorite Holmes novel of the canon. Aside from my particular love of this novel, though, it's also often the main (and sometimes only) view people have into the canon. It's frequently required reading in schools, there have been a ton of films made of it, and it's one of the most referenced stories in popular culture. The iconic image of Holmes in his deerstalker cap and long coat comes from this story as well (although it's still only referred to as a "cloth cap" — the deerstalker came from later illustrations of the story). So naturally, there's a lot to talk about in this novel.

Holmes

This story is generally seen as a classic example of Holmes at the top of his game — great deductions from physical evidence, a few key facts gleaned from inconsistencies from personal statements, and even an example of him using his ability of disguise to progress the case. However, he makes mistakes in his deductions; he is still a flawed detective. I've noticed that this is common in the longer Holmes stories: the more words there are devoted to a case (or at least Holmes' portion of the case), the more mistakes he makes. This isn't always true, but it is a trend in a variety of Holmes stories, both canonical and pastiche.

One good example of this is in chapter four, when he makes a mistake in regards to trying to capture the man in the cab, although he immediately explains to Watson how he should have accomplished it. Doyle causes Holmes to fail for narrative expedience (as the case would have been readily solved if he had captured the man), but he has Holmes immediately detail his mistake so that his powers of quick reasoning are kept intact. For a while in my life, I thought this was pretty clunky and implausible, but over the years there have been a number of times where I've done something and then immediately recognized my mistake and how I should have done things differently. Now this scene makes Holmes feel quite human to me — even this masterful genius sometimes kicks himself immediately after making a blunder, just like we do.

We learn a bit more about Holmes' thought process in chapter three, where he mentions that a "concentrated atmosphere helps a concentration of thought." We also find out in chapter fifteen why Holmes has such an extensive collection of notes: because "[i]ntense mental concentration has a curious way of blotting out what has passed," and therefore he is unlikely to keep the facts of one case in his head when he is on another case. (This brings up the question of why he is able to reference past cases mentally and so frequently. Perhaps certain "details of interest" stay in his memory while the more mundane details get "blotted out?")

Holmes' knowledge of art comes up again in *Hound* on two different occasions. First, Watson chides him in chapter five.

He would talk of nothing but art, of which he had the crudest ideas...

In previous stories, Holmes has been portrayed as having either a masterful knowledge of art or no knowledge at all. In this story, both sides seem to be blended a bit, with Watson taking a slightly snobbish attitude toward Holmes' knowledge. Holmes fires back at this observation in chapter thirteen, turning the whole continuity concern into a nice character detail of their friendship.

"Watson won't allow that I know anything of art but that is mere jealousy because our views upon the subject differ."

We also learn that Holmes is very fastidious, as Watson mentions "...that catlike love of personal cleanliness which was one of his characteristics...." He also does not laugh very often, although he does so in this story. Watson reaffirms Holmes' flair for the dramatic, citing it as one of his flaws.

Finally, there is a very touching moment in chapter five where we see Holmes' concern for Watson.

"I can only wish you better luck in Devonshire. But I'm not easy in my mind about it."

"About what?"

"About sending you. It's an ugly business, Watson, an ugly dangerous business, and the more I see of it the less I like it. Yes my dear fellow, you may laugh, but I give you my word that I shall be very glad to have you back safe and sound in Baker Street once more."

Watson

Watson's intelligence is displayed inconsistently in this story, and is best summarized by Holmes himself.

"I am bound to say that in all the accounts which you have been so good as to give of my own small achievements you have habitually underrated your own abilities. It may be that you are not yourself luminous, but you are a conductor of light. Some people without possessing genius have a remarkable power of stimulating it. I confess, my dear fellow, that I am very much in your debt."

Watson makes some deductions which turn out to be wrong, and the mild sarcasm from Holmes above is his reward for such. The scene with the walking stick is similar to the scene with the hat in "The Blue Carbuncle," but instead of Watson seeing much and admitting he doesn't see anything, this time he dives right into the bad deductions. He gets better throughout the story, especially when he is left on his own in Baskerville Hall and gathers some good information about the people around him. He even manipulates Frankland in much the same way that Holmes manipulated the goose vender in "Carbuncle." But despite it all, his contributions toward collecting the data necessary for the case are diminished under Holmes' deductions derived from that same data.

In fact, one of the best things about the narrative structure of *Hound* is that Holmes is actually missing for several chapters, leaving Watson fully in the front of the story. Although the novel ends up taking many of Watson's observations and showing them to be incorrect (which is, to be fair, an important part of the mystery novel structure), this is the story in which I really began to believe that Watson was talented as a detective in his own right. If you break each deduction made in the story down, some of Holmes' initial deductions are wrong while several of Watson's are later verified, even though all the ones Watson directly tells Holmes are dismissed. Regardless of his success or failure as a detective, though, he is peerless as a man of action and integrity; he is brave and loyal throughout the book, not only to Holmes but to Sir Charles Baskerville.

Doyle not only leaves Watson alone for several chapters, but he changes the formula up even more by framing some of the Watson-only chapters as letters and diary entries, which give a little more insight into Watson's own head. We learn that Watson isn't a deep sleeper, although this is in direct conflict with *A Study in Scarlet* where he says "I get up at all sorts of ungodly hours," but supported by his comment in "The Speckled Band" where he says he is "regular in my habits" — it's possible that as he recovered from his injuries in Afghanistan that he ended up becoming more of an early riser, but all of the statements taken at face value seem to contradict each other. We also see that he is desperate for Holmes' approval in his frequent requests for congratulations. While Watson has previously seemed inclined to at least consider supernatural options, he doesn't see himself as a superstitious man, claiming that "if I have one quality upon earth it is common sense." There's even a nice reference back to the very earliest part of their friendship in *A Study in Scarlet*:

"I can still remember your complete indifference as to whether the sun moved round the earth or the earth round the sun."

But unlike *Scarlet* (where Holmes is also missing for a large part of the book), in *Hound* Watson's constant references to how his friend would handle things or making sure that he makes Holmes proud keeps Holmes in the narrative even when he isn't present. You never feel like it stops being a story about Holmes, because Watson always references or evokes his friend. Even the act of framing some chapters as letters to Holmes keeps us grounded in the fact that he is important to these events, and Watson's tender references to his friend in those letters also reminds us of the special relationship the two men share.

When they are reunited in chapter twelve, Watson is furious with Holmes for using him. Holmes admits that Watson's humanity and loyalty are sometimes inconvenient to his work.

"But why keep me in the dark?"

"For you to know could not have helped us and might possibly have led to my discovery. You would have wished to tell me something, or in your kindness you would have brought me out some comfort or other, and so an unnecessary risk would be run..."

This scene in chapter twelve shows that these two men have a real relationship — they fight, they argue, they insult and deride each other, and yet they care very much and are loyal to each other.

Everything Else

As I mentioned earlier, *Hound* is probably one of the most influential books in the Holmes canon. Entire books have been written about just this novel, including *Sherlock Holmes was Wrong* by Pierre Bayard, which attempts to refute just about every point in the case. More than twenty films over the course of a century have been made adapting the novel, with varying degrees of faithfulness to the original. It was the first ever "Book Club" discussion at the first 221b Con, and everyone was able to dive in and discuss it at length. There's even a medical contribution named after the book — the "Hound of the Baskervilles effect" is the observation that the fatality of a heart attack is increased by psychological stress, especially stress imposed by the victim's supernatural beliefs. (Seriously. It's in the *British Medical Journal*. 2001 December 22; 323(7327): 1443—1446. If you're interested.)

Part of the reason why this story resonates so strongly is that it addresses a strong theme in the Holmes canon — the conflict between superstition and scientific observation — over and over throughout the book. Although later stories like "The Sussex Vampire" also address superstition, this book constantly dances over the line, evoking the Gothic ghost stories popular in the 19th century and convincing the audience that Holmes might have found his match in the supernatural, before pulling back the curtain and showing everyone that there's a perfectly logical (if convoluted) reason for everything. Holmes' conflict with the supernatural is a rich area for countless pastiches since, including one of my favorites, *The Italian Secretary* by Caleb Carr (which is probably the most like *Hound* in terms of structure and how the supernatural incidents resolve themselves).

As much as the book talks about Victorian superstition, it brings to light one element of Victorian science as well. In chapter one, Holmes is referred to being second-best only to "Monsieur Bertillon." This is actually Alphonse Bertillon, the French creator of the Bertillon system, which is the first-ever scientific system of criminal identification. His method relied on physical measurements of suspects to clarify and support eye-witness data. Part of his system involved taking pictures of suspects from the front and from the side to give a better sense of their appearance, and example photos from the time look identical to the mug shots that police still use today. The system turned out to be flawed — so much so that some of the flaws ended up being fodder for one of the stories of the "gentleman thief" Arsene Lupin, written by Doyle's French counterpart, Maurice Leblanc. No wonder Holmes chafes at being considered inferior to Bertillon...

But what would a Holmes story be without a chronology tangle? Even devoted Sherlockian scholars have trouble dating the case. The references I have access to date it anywhere from September 28, 1886 to September 25, 1900 — a span of fourteen years! *Hound* starts off with no reference to "The Final Problem," which implies the case is set before Holmes' death. The whole story feels very pre-marriage (especially since Watson doesn't mention his wife once), and that's reinforced by Holmes asking Watson to stay when the client arrives — a very early aspect of their relationship. Watson's failure in developing correct deductions from the walking stick also points to an earlier phase in their relationship. However, that same stick is dated 1884, which is "five years ago," making the date 1889 — one year after Watson's marriage!

Holmes' claim to have handled five hundred cases by this point doesn't help us as much as one would hope in dating the case — at first glance, it seems to indicate the half-way point in Holmes' career, since in "The Final Problem" he boasted of a thousand cases solved. It's likely, though, that he started off with a few cases here and there, and then gained more and more as his popularity grew, so the time of going from five hundred cases to one thousand is probably much shorter than it was going from one to five hundred. But five hundred cases from 1889 to 1891 is quite a lot, even for Holmes.

Aside from chronology, there are a handful of other interesting points to think about in the novel. Remember how I mentioned that Lestrade is marginalized and ignored throughout the first part of the canon? He comes back in *Hound*, and we see where Lestrade gets his canonical longevity. Not only does his appearance here in this widely-known story increase his exposure to the eyes of casual Holmes readers, but Lestrade is also given a lot more room as a character. He is mentioned as "the best of the professionals," a far cry from Holmes' original opinion of him. Some of that may be because Lestrade is now reverential to

Holmes, and is noted as learning much from the master detective. As a result, it's likely that Lestrade has become less aggressive and antagonistic towards Holmes over time, and this increased Holmes' opinion of Lestrade. We also get some more details about him, as he is described as a "wiry bulldog" and a "little detective."

We encounter more phrenology in this story, in what is probably one of my favorite lines in the book:

"I had hardly expected so dolichocephalic a skull or such well-marked supra-orbital development. Would you have any objection to my running my finger along your parietal fissure? A cast of your skull, sir, until the original is available, would be an ornament to any anthropological museum. It is not my intention to be fulsome, but I confess that I covet your skull."

(For a bit of fun, compare the physical description of Dr. James Mortimer in this story and the description of Professor James Moriarty in "The Final Problem." And both do seem to be well-versed in phrenology....)

Doyle continues his trend of apocryphal cases, this time having Holmes refer to "the little affair of the Vatican cameos" and his work for "one of the most revered names in England," as well as two more in the final chapter. There's also a reference to a previous case in which Holmes works with Cartright, which shows an interesting narrative component to all these apocryphal cases — they not only continue to paint a picture of Holmes' wider career in a world outside of the stories we are reading, but also doubles as a nice way to quickly introduce a minor character into the narrative.

There's a second instance of someone making a note on their shirt-cuff. We also see another case of brain-fever when Baskerville snaps near the end of the story. There's another butler as a suspect, but this one is falsely accused (as opposed to the one in "The Musgrave Ritual"). Doyle's peppering of "gipsys" in the canon continues, this time with a passing reference to Murphy, the horse-dealer. We have another villain that escapes mortal law, only to be claimed by natural justice (in this case, the moor).

All in all, this is a classic story in the Holmes canon. It hits a lot of key elements for the main characters as well as the canon as a whole. Many of the themes and tropes you see throughout the canon are presented in *The Hound of the Baskervilles*, so it's no wonder that it's often viewed as the archetypal Sherlock Holmes story. I cannot recommend it enough as a novel (although many individual stories are better, in my opinion).

The Return of Sherlock Holmes

The Adventure of the Empty House (1903)

It has been ten years since Doyle wrote "The Final Problem," but only three years have elapsed in Watson's world — the case is set in the spring of 1894. Doyle makes an attempt to explain the time by having Watson claim that Holmes asked him to remain silent until ten years had passed, but the reason why Watson was asked to remain silent isn't really explained here (although it could be in relation to Holmes' eventual retirement in 1903). Here, Doyle goes back to an old favorite structure of his: the locked-room mystery. Of course, the actual mystery isn't really focused on much here, because the story is really just a vehicle to reintroduce Holmes, so it's paced more like an adventure story than a mystery. As a result, Doyle's skill over past ten years of from writing exactly those kinds of adventure stories is showcased in this story.

We learn that Watson has taken up the science of detection in the absence of his friend. We don't get a sense of whether he was particularly good at it or not, and we don't ever really get any information about the time in which Watson acted on his own, but the fact that Watson did so for three years indicates to me that he wasn't particularly bad at it, either — for example, although he didn't see Moriarty's men, he did find the undercover policemen quite easily. Perhaps some of Holmes' methods did actually rub off on Watson after all. We also learn that Watson has only ever fainted once in his life: when Holmes returns from the dead.

There's also an interesting wrinkle in Watson's missing wife. Watson doesn't mention his wife at all during any of this, but does make a very small reference to "my own sad bereavement." Many Sherlockians take this to mean that his wife has died, and I tend to agree — it explains a lot of things in coming stories. It also may explain why he doesn't mention her in previous stories: if she died somewhere between 1892 and 1894, then Watson may have not wanted to write about his wife so soon after losing her. More likely, Doyle was recovering from the loss of his own wife, and writing about even a fictional marriage may have been too painful.

When Holmes explains where he's been for three years, he mentions his mastery of baritsu, or the art of Japanese wrestling. Baritsu doesn't actually exist, but it's been referenced by other writers since this story, and pulp staples such as The Shadow and Doc Savage were masters the art as well. There *is* a real Victorian martial art called *bartitsu* (with two "t"s) that is based around self-defense, but it wasn't invented until 1898, which would have been four years after Holmes' return. Further, it wasn't created by the Japanese at all, but rather by an Englishman as a composite of various Japanese martial arts. Odds are that Doyle heard about bartitsu, didn't see how it was spelled, and decided to use it. However, the fictional martial art was far more popular than its real-life component, with bartitsu quickly fading into obscurity until it was rediscovered in the 1950s by (of course) a Sherlockian. In the past several years the art has made quite a comeback, and bartitsu schools are flourishing all over the world.

Mycroft had been acting as Holmes' agent in London while he was away, even to the point of keeping his rooms preserved, despite the fact that his rooms were *set on fire* during "The Final Problem." Though Holmes was conducting business in London through his brother, he intentionally kept Watson unaware of his existence for three years. Once again, Holmes lies to Watson (albeit a lie of omission) because he is afraid Watson will talk, but he doesn't have the same concern about his brother's ability to keep a confidence. I sometimes debate if Holmes' mistrust of Watson's ability to stay quiet is more telling of Holmes' inability to trust anyone or of Watson's inability to keep a secret. I'm more inclined toward the former, since we've seen multiple instances of where Watson is able to lie to others and keep secrets, and we have seen Holmes trust Watson in many other ways, even with his life. Some have suggested that it stems from Holmes' passive-aggressive hatred of Watson's published accounts, which is as good a theory as any. But no matter how you look at it, Holmes is being really damned cruel to Watson here, and Watson is far too forgiving of it.

The time between 1891 and 1894 (referred to by Sherlockians as "The Great Hiatus") is the subject of a wide variety of speculation and interest. Some have debated whether Holmes could have even been in the places he claimed to be, while others have attributed all manner of fictional and real world events to Holmes during that time. More outlandish theories flourish, including Holmes actually dying and being replaced with a long-lost cousin, a sister, and even a part of Holmes' own soul that was split off from him in Russia! *The New Annotated Sherlock Holmes, Vol. II* devotes seven whole pages to the topic, and the editor admits that it's just a small sample of discussion on The Great Hiatus. (One scholar, A. Carson Simpson, wrote four volumes on the topic!)

While Moriarty is mentioned in this story, we actually don't learn a whole lot more about him directly, aside from the manner of his demise (which is more definitive than Holmes').

107

We do, however, meet his right-hand man, Colonel Sebastian Moran. While not quite on the same level of cultural notoriety as Moriarty himself, Moran certainly enjoys a lot of popularity with pastiche writers. The idea of the criminal subordinate has influenced a lot of fiction over the past century. Moran is often placed in a Watson-like role to Moriarty, continuing the "evil twin" structure. Kim Newman does this to wonderfully comedic effect in his short story collection *The Hound of the D'urbervilles*, which parodies not only several Sherlock Holmes stories, but also more 19th century books than I could possibly identify without using Google.

One thing I particularly like is that a throw-away line in "The Final Problem" (where Holmes cryptically mentions air guns and never elaborates on it) becomes the core of this story. Sure, Doyle has done a lot of cross-references between the stories before, but this is the first time in which an unexplained piece of previous story was actually followed up in a later one.

Other interesting canonical bits:

- Another case showcasing Lestrade. He really does dominate the middle of the canon a lot more than I remembered.
- There are two more references in the story pointing to the theory of genetic criminal disposition: "…without reading Nature's plainest danger-signals" and "…such a sudden turn to good or evil stands for some strong influence which came into the line of his pedigree." Ah, Victorian science.
- Mrs. Hudson is mentioned twice. It's around this time in the canon where she gets more prominence, much like Lestrade.

- Holmes dons his mouse-colored dressing gown. He's done this a few times before, but this is probably its most iconic appearance. In my mind, this brown gown is far more "Holmes" than the deerstalker and coat.
- We learn that Holmes is actually missing his left canine from a situation in a previous case: "...and Mathews, who knocked out my left canine in the waiting-room at Charing Cross...." The fact that Watson has never mentioned it implies that Holmes may have gotten a replacement at some point.

The Adventure of the Norwood Builder (1903)

And now we start the post-Great Hiatus canon proper with "The Norwood Builder." In short order Holmes bemoans the loss of Moriarty, while Watson sells his medical practice and moves in with Holmes (another good indication that Watson's wife may be deceased by this point). Holmes and Watson living as bachelors at 221B Baker Street is what many people envision when they think of the canon, and it makes sense from Doyle's perspective to move things back to that relationship. That means that we now have six rough bands of time in the canon: Holmes pre-practice, Holmes pre-Watson (after he started acting as a detective), Holmes and Watson pre-marriage, Holmes and Watson post-marriage, the Great Hiatus, and now Holmes and Watson post-Hiatus (and pre-retirement). This story is obviously post-Hiatus, but in future it'll be hard to distinguish between pre-marriage and post-Hiatus, since the structures for both are very similar.

Early on in the story there are references to two apocryphal cases ("...the case of the papers of ex-President Murillo and also the shocking affair of the Dutch steamship

Friesland…"), but the former is actually another situation where Doyle repurposed an apocryphal case and turned it into a canonical one — in this case, "Wisteria Lodge." Interestingly, the latter reference *was* used in another Doyle story, but not a Holmes one. In fact, the *S.S. Friesland* was mentioned in the classic Professor Challenger novel *The Lost World* about the discovery of living dinosaurs, which would certainly be a "shocking affair" to Watson!

We learn a little more of Holmes' family, as Watson's practice is purchased by a Dr. Verner, who turns out to be a "distant relation" to Holmes. This has, naturally, led to a lot of speculation about Holmes' family tree as a result, but given that we know both Holmes brothers are bachelors, it's likely that they had an aunt or uncle with their own family, or perhaps even a great-aunt or great-uncle.

Much like Holmes was in early pre-marriage canon, he is resistant to notoriety and praise, especially with his admonishment to Watson to not publish any account of his cases for ten years:

His cold and proud nature was always averse, however, to anything in the shape of public applause, and he bound me in the most stringent terms to say no further word of himself, his methods, or his successes....

Holmes himself repeats this admonishment to Lestrade later in the story. In both cases, the implication is that Holmes has always been this way (and indeed, his own swipes as Watson's publication of cases before the Great Hiatus bears this out), but it raises the question of why Holmes is so adamant against public praise, especially considering he is self-admittedly theatrical (even in this story) and clearly enjoys individual praise.

On the other hand, Holmes is not so careful about hiding his excitement when a more delicate response is called for:

"This is really most grati — most interesting."

as later:

My companion's expressive face showed a sympathy which was not, I am afraid, entirely unmixed with satisfaction.

Watson again proves he is quite adept in making deductions. After Holmes does his usual breakdown of McFarlane's occupation, health problems, and marital status just by looking at him, Watson follows up with his own work:

... it was not difficult for me to follow his deductions, and to observe the untidiness of attire, the sheaf of legal papers, the watch-charm, and the breathing which had prompted them.

Good for Watson!

This story reinforces Lestrade's place in the canon. Much like *Hound*, he has a great deal of space in this story, and the friendly and respectful rivalry between the two men is borne out well in this story. Holmes even gives Lestrade a back-handed compliment when he says "You do not add imagination to your other great qualities..." Holmes is quite flustered when there's a chance that Lestrade might actually be correct on the case, which is a rare occurrence. Lestrade takes some swipes at Holmes during the case, which Holmes returns at the end, but each side takes the jibs well in both cases, showing a level of respect and appreciation between Holmes and the official force that the earlier canon didn't display.

This is also the first Holmes story in which fingerprinting is a key clue. At this point fingerprint recognition is a very new scientific theory in criminology, which is why the concept is explained excessively during the story. Fingerprinting eventually takes over the Bertillon system that was popular at the time (Scotland Yard formally adopts a fingerprinting bureau in 1901), so it's interesting to see Doyle using such a new-fangled theory as fingerprinting in this story.

Despite the awkward ending (surely even Scotland Yard can tell the difference between human bones and rabbit bones!), you can see that Doyle has fallen back into a good rhythm in writing Holmes. This is a good mystery all around, and seeing Holmes in a position where he might actually lose the case is quite convincing. Another great story in the canon.

The Adventure of the Dancing Men (1903)

First, a caveat. This is the first short story in which pictures are an important part of the story. The story revolves around the cypher of the dancing men. It's possible to read the story without the pictures, but some of the references (like the mention of the flags) really don't make sense without the pictures in front of you. Annoyingly, some public domain versions of the story don't have the pictures, so if you're using a free or online source to read these stories, there's a chance that you might be missing something important. *Caveat emptor* and all that.

This story has a good section with Holmes explaining some basic cryptography — in this case, a substitution cypher. One thing I like about this story is that it starts off as a fairly light and fun puzzle about some child-like drawings that suddenly turns into a dark locked-room mystery. (Doyle seemed to love locked room puzzles and American wives with mysterious pasts). While Holmes does win in the end, he does so to gain revenge instead of preventing tragedy — certainly a mixed success at best.

The opening scene where Holmes deduces Watson's thoughts by observation (again!) gives a few more brush-strokes of Watson's character: he has a friend named Thurston and a fondness for billiards. We also learn later that Holmes has a friend in the New York police force named Hargreave, which implies that Holmes may have been to America before, either before he met Watson or during the Great Hiatus.

The case timing is pretty vague, but there is one reference to "the Jubilee." It could be Victoria's Golden Jubilee (1887) or the Diamond Jubilee (1897). That puts the case at either 1888 or 1898. Given Watson's surprise at Holmes' methods early on in the story, this could mean the case is in 1888, making it pre-marriage, but most scholars accept it as being set in 1898.

The Adventure of the Solitary Cyclist (1903)

"The Solitary Cyclist" is one of Doyle's weaker stories, by Doyle's own admission. In fact, the *Strand* magazine almost didn't pick it up because Holmes isn't very involved in the plot of the story (although Watson is, so it's a bonus for Watson fans like myself). To paraphrase Holmes himself, though, it does have one or two points of interest.

A lot of Holmes' character quirks are reaffirmed in this story. He hates distractions when he's concentrating, he references his skill with boxing, and Holmes has a preference for clapping a pistol to a criminal's head (so much so that he encourages Watson to perform the same maneuver against Williamson). One thing that is expanded upon is the conflicting stances on Watson's capabilities as a detective. On the one hand, Watson's observations in this late-canonical period continue to be keen:

...I observed the slight roughening of the side of the sole caused by the friction of the edge of the pedal.

After Holmes sends Watson to investigate Miss Violet Smith's "trifling intrigue," he is incredibly critical of Watson's failure to produce results — which Watson doesn't take well:

"What should I have done?" I cried, with some heat.

"Gone to the nearest public-house. That is the center of country gossip. They would have told you every name, from the master to the scullery-maid. Williamson! It conveys nothing to my mind. If he is an elderly man he is not this active cyclist who sprints away from that athletic young lady's pursuit. What have we gained by your expedition? The knowledge that the girl's story is true. I never doubted it. That there is a connection between the cyclist and the Hall. I never doubted that either. That the Hall is tenanted by Williamson. Who's the better for that?"

There's also a conflict over exactly how much exercise each man gets regularly. When Holmes gets beaten up, he says that it's a treat because he gets little active exercise. However, later on Watson says that Holmes is always in training. Watson himself claims that he loses ground to Holmes in a foot chase because he has led a sedentary life, but at the very start of the story he says that from the years 1894 to 1901 Sherlock Holmes was a very busy man, and near the end points out that they don't often

114

see the resolution of cases because one case tends to roll right into the next one. (Further, in *Hound*, Watson claims that he and Sir Henry were "very swift runners.") These aren't completely contradictory statements — what Holmes considers active exercise and what Watson considers training may differ, and Watson may have been sedentary through many of the cases — but there's certainly some confusion on their activity level. I suspect stories like this one, though, are another instance of what led to the image of "fat Watson".

Speaking of exercise, this story showcases the late Victorian fad of bicycling. From about 1870 to 1890, Victorians were obsessed with bicycling, with thousands of bicycles being sold every year. Not only was it a great leisure activity, but it also allowed poorer workers to increase their range of employment options (having previously only been relegated to the distance they could walk), and offered some freedom to young people of the time. While some considered bicycles to be a great boon, others worried of the immorality of young women riding alone for miles to visit barely-known male acquaintances. Based on the time period and pictures from the *Strand*, it appears that the bicycles mentioned are the "safety" bicycles with two equal-sized wheels that we are familiar with today, rather than the earlier "penny farthing" bicycles that you see in episodes of *The Prisoner* or poorly-researched steampunk novels.

Some other canonical tropes are also reaffirmed in this story. There are more references to apocryphal cases (such as the one with Archie Stamford, the forger), Watson continues to lament that London is drab and gray and speaks glowingly of the beauty of nature, and we see another instance of someone using a black beard as a disguise (the last time was in *Hound*). On the other hand, there are a couple of new things that come out, such as the concept that private citizens could take criminals into "personal custody" until the proper authorities arrived. It is also one of the few instances in British literature of the time of a case of forced marriage or bride kidnapping — while the bulk of the story intimates that the criminals are forcing themselves on Miss Smith for her inheritance, there is also an undercurrent of forced sex that runs through the story.

Finally, even such an explicit example of case timing is still in dispute. The story allegedly starts on Saturday, April 23, 1895. However, April 23, 1895 was a Tuesday. Sometimes I wonder if Doyle is just trolling everyone.

The Adventure of the Priory School (1904)

Amusingly, although the last story was about a cyclist, this story has the most enduring controversy about bicycles — specifically, bicycle tire (or, more accurately, "tyre") tracks. William S. Baring-Gould, one of the most respected Sherlockian scholars, complained "Much, perhaps too much, has been written about these tyre tracks." So let's write some more about them.

The controversy comes from the scene in which Holmes deduces which direction a bicycle was riding based on the impressions the tires left in the mud (specifically, how the weight of the rear wheel obliterates the front wheel impressions). I admit my own reaction on reading this was "it should be obliterated the same way regardless of what direction the bike's going," and that seems to be the conclusion of a number of Sherlockians.

The correspondence on this point was so intense even in Doyle's time that he remarked on it in his autobiography *Memoirs and Adventures*. Doyle was tired of the criticism and tried to refute it by conducting tests with his own bicycle, and found that while his correspondents were correct about that specific observation, there were other ways to tell which way the bicycle was headed. A number of other Sherlockians have pointed out similar evidence to determine a bicycle's direction independent of the depth of the tire's impression. In the end, Doyle was actually wrong and admitted as such, but the idea that Holmes was able to deduce which direction the bicycle was going in is still sound.

This is the third story in a row that starts off light and entertaining (in this case, the humorous entrance of Thorneycroft Huxtable, M.A., Ph.D., which is probably the most awesome name in the entire canon), but turns into a more somber and darker affair. Watson occasionally smokes cigarettes (they're only mentioned twice: in this story and in *Hound*) and Holmes banks at The Capital and Counties Bank, Oxford Street branch. We get more tantalizing glimpses into apocryphal cases, such as the case of the Ferrers Documents and the Abergavenny murder. We even learn a bit about the strict legal nature of noble inheritance.

But one of the more interesting points is the lengthy discussion between Holmes and the Duke at the end of the story. Holmes again demonstrates that his own moral opinions on justice supersede a literal interpretation of the law:

"I must take the view, your Grace, that when a man embarks upon a crime he is morally guilty of any other crime which may spring from it."

This is consistent with our view of Holmes from previous stories, such as "The Blue Carbuncle." While he refuses to take the Duke's subtle bribe of twelve thousand pounds to keep silent, he is not only persistent about collecting the promised six thousand pounds, but marks the cheque as being more interesting than the obfuscatory horseshoes from the Middle Ages which nearly defeated him. He comes across as uncharacteristically mercenary, but I think it's consistent. Holmes is very much a man that is happy to implement his own justice on people, and in this case he may have thought that taking the Duke's money (which amounts to over $100,000 in current spending power) might have been the only kind of punishment he would have understood. But even I confess that's somewhat sketchy logic — the whole scene doesn't match up well with what we know of Holmes, but it does feel more like we're uncovering new depths of his character rather than seeing an inconsistency of vision.

Yes, there's more confusion about case timing. Given that there's a reference that the Duke of Holdernesse had been Lord Lieutenant of Hallamshire "since 1900" and a mention of May 13th implies that the case is probably set in 1901, which is the outer edge of the post-Hiatus timeframe. However, in "The Blanched Soldier" (coming up), Holmes himself mentioned he was "clearing up the case which my friend Watson has described as that of the Abbey School, in which the Duke of Greyminster was so deeply involved." This sounds very much like this case (albeit with a different Duke's name), but "The Blanched Soldier" is set in 1903!

But for once, I'm not going to let that bother me, because this story has a great quote about Huxtable which shows Doyle's under-appreciated comic style:

We had sprung to our feet, and for a few moments we stared in silent amazement at this ponderous piece of wreckage, which told of some sudden and fatal storm far out on the ocean of life.

The Adventure of Black Peter (1904)

In the first week of July 1895, Watson claims that Holmes was at the top of his game mentally and physically. It's a good piece of data on Holmes' career, as well as a great way to date this story, "Black Peter." For a story about Holmes at the top of his game, we certainly see a lot of old favorites played to good effect. Holmes takes on the case based on their challenger rather than because of the status or wealth of the client, although Watson does point out that the only exception to this is when Holmes demanded a large reward at the end of the previous story, "The Priory School." Holmes manages one end of the investigation in disguise (and without telling Watson anything about it), and another long night-time vigil leads to the capture of a key component of the case.

But this story does bring a few new pieces to light. Watson mentions that it would be an indiscretion to even hint at some of the clients Holmes has had, and yet he name-drops the Pope. (This is apparently the second time Holmes has worked for the Pope, too — the first was mentioned in *Hound of the Baskervilles*.) We find out that Holmes has five small refuges all around London in which to change into a disguise — a fact that has led to much baseless speculation among Sherlockians as to their actual locations. Watson admits that it's not his habit to force a confidence, although he comes quite near to forcing one with Baskerville in *Hound*.

We also meet a new police inspector, Stanley Hopkins, "...for whose future Holmes held high hopes." Hopkins is far more deferential and in awe of Holmes' methods than any of the other policemen we've met in the canon, but Holmes is still flippant and harsh with Hopkins.

"I know your methods, sir, and I applied them. Before I permitted anything to be moved I examined most carefully the ground outside, and also the floor of the room. There were no footmarks."

"Meaning that you saw none?"

"I assure you, sir, that there were none."

"My good Hopkins, I have investigated many crimes, but I have never yet seen one which was committed by a flying creature."

Over time, Hopkins becomes convinced that he's acquired the real criminal, and Holmes moves from flippant to disappointed. Even though Hopkins eventually admits that "...I am the pupil and you are the master," Holmes never really gives Hopkins much of a break. This relationship is interesting because it's a contrast to the relationship Holmes has with Lestrade (in which Holmes is politely dismissive of Lestrade's ham-fisted methods), but similar to his relationship with Watson (in which Holmes is intensely critical of any of Watson's deductions). Holmes is harder on people he sees potential in or is fond of, and more tolerant around people he thinks very little of.

There are some interesting bits of Doyle's style (good and bad) to dig into here as well. He nicely sets up the vital clue of the case right at the beginning of the story, with the anecdote of Holmes attempting to stab through a pig. It's another attempt to "play fair" with the reader, as much of the evidence that Holmes used in his deduction is available to the reader as well. Conversely, the capture of Patrick Cairns is nearly identical to the capture of Jefferson Hope in *A Study in Scarlet*. We also get another glimpse into the workings of the Victorian Stock Exchange (the first was in "The Stock-Broker's Clerk"), but we're left with a sudden and unexplained trip for Holmes and Watson to Norway. Why the need for the trip? There's a lot of confusion on that point as far as I can tell, and I don't see a case in the canon where the reference links up to.

Also, I really like the word "ambuscade":

It was past eleven o'clock when we formed our little ambuscade.

The Adventure of Charles Augustus Milverton (1904)

Right up front, Watson is clear about the fact that he's concealing the date and the facts to help place this "absolutely unique experience." Despite the constant disappointments I have in trying to reconcile the dates of the cases, this intentional obfuscation just encourages me to dig more than usual to try to place it.

First off, we're in the iconic situation of Watson living as a bachelor with Holmes, so we know it's not during Watson's marriage or the Great Hiatus. Holmes at one point claims that he's had to deal with "fifty murderers" in his career at this point, which could indicate it's right before Watson's marriage, but that's no real help. There's a reference to electric light switches which I thought could be a clue, but they were invented in 1884, so that doesn't help either.

Turning to history, though, we get more information. There was a real-life blackmailer named Charles Augustus Howell who died in 1890. If we assume that "Milverton" was simply a very clumsy cover for "Howell," then we have a year — 1890, right before the Great Hiatus. Many Sherlockians (including Baring-Gould) place the case in 1899, for reasons I wasn't able to uncover. So I flipped a table and moved on.

Aside from whether this case is before or after Holmes matches wits with Professor Moriarty, however, there's a lot of similar tensions between Holmes and Milverton. Holmes considers Milverton to be "the worst man in London," a description he usually reserves for Moriarty. But it does seem that Holmes has a particular hatred of blackmailers — he is quite passionate on the subject. It opens up some interesting speculations about Holmes' past. Was Holmes or someone in his past blackmailed? Regardless, there's a great battle of wits between Holmes and Milverton, and Milverton turns out to be quite clever and well-prepared. He's a great villain, perhaps on par with Moriarty himself. In fact, Holmes' outrage with blackmailers in general and Milverton in specific leads him to take drastic actions. He fakes an engagement to a housemaid to get information, and his comment about a "hated rival" in her affections feels like a flimsy justification for his blatant manipulation. He hates blackmailers, but he's happy to toy with a woman's affections in pursuit of his case.

Even worse, he's willing to break and enter into Milverton's home, which he also attempts to justify:

"I suppose that you will admit that the action is morally justifiable, though technically criminal. To burgle his house is no more than to forcibly take his pocket-book — an action in which you were prepared to aid me."

Further, he tries to claim that he's willing to do it because "a lady is in the most desperate need of his help." However, he certainly had no problems toying with another woman's emotions! Because one is a servant and another is a lady, though, some have pointed to this as an example of Holmes' class bias. I don't buy it, though. I think the reality is much simpler: it's all about Holmes' pride:

"Between ourselves, Watson, it's a sporting duel between this fellow Milverton and me. He had, as you saw, the best of the first exchanges; but my self-respect and my reputation are concerned to fight it to a finish."

Watson seems strangely reluctant to have Holmes break the law here, even though he wasn't at all resistant to breaking into a house in "The Bruce-Partington Plans." But despite this inconsistency, it leads to a great exchange between Holmes and Watson, possibly one of my favorites:

"Well, I don't like it; but I suppose it must be," said I. "When do we start?"

"You are not coming."

"Then you are not going," said I. "I give you my word of honor — and I never broke it in my life — that I will take a cab straight to the police-station and give you away unless you let me share this adventure with you."

"You can't help me."

"How do you know that? You can't tell what may happen. Anyway, my resolution is taken. Other people beside you have self-respect and even reputations."

Holmes had looked annoyed, but his brow cleared, and he clapped me on the shoulder.

"Well, well, my dear fellow, be it so. We have shared the same room for some years, and it would be amusing if we ended by sharing the same cell."

There are other interesting bits to learn in this story. Holmes has a particular hobby of opening safes, and thus has a state-of-the-art burgling kit on hand. He can see in the dark, and has "quicker senses" than Watson. Watson is strangely thrilled by the law-breaking, even when he tries to justify it by going on about the "high object of our mission." Watson seems to understand a lot of Holmes' ideas from a handshake and a grasp of his wrist; they are very much in sync. Watson also owns tennis shoes, and runs for two miles — looks like his days of his leg injury are long behind him. And it's implied that Lestrade is learning a lot from Holmes, not taking Holmes' pat explanation of Watson's break-in at face value.

There are some problems with the story. There isn't really a mystery here — Holmes and Watson are really just observers and vigilantes, and we never really learn who the "noble statesmen" whose wife murdered Milverton was. But it is a great story, both in general and as another example of Doyle's dry wit mixed with grisly situations.

The Adventure of the Six Napoleons (1904)

Before I dig into this story, I should really start by talking about the Victorian concept of "monomania." Watson mentions this as a possible explanation of the destruction of the Napoleon busts, also referring to the French concept "idée fix." Monomania was a psychological disorder that seems to crop up a fair amount in Victorian literature. Poe used it extensively in his own work (perhaps most famously in "The Tell-Tale Heart"), it comes up a couple of times in the works of Honore de Balzac, and Captain Ahab in *Moby-Dick* is a classic case of the monomaniac. Like the ever-popular brain fever, monomania is a great literary device, perhaps out of all proportion for the actual illness.

Other historical references in this story circle around Italian life in Victorian London. There's a reference to "Saffron Hill" in the story, which is one of two Italian communities in London at the time (the other was in Soho). It's the Victorian equivalent of "Little Italy." There's also a reference to the black pearl of the Borgias, which were a notorious Italian family (although, as far as I can tell, the pearl itself is fictional). Finally, Holmes mentions the Mafia. Doyle characterizes it as a "secret political society," and it certainly had a disproportional amount of influence in the politics of Italy at the time, but it was just as involved in more mainstream criminal activity, such as theft, kidnapping, and counterfeiting. Reading about the Mafia, though, has the same kind of cognitive dissonance for as reading about the KKK in "Five Orange Pips."

Oh, and the story contains perhaps the first ever fictional incident of deliberate news manipulation.

Lestrade features in this story, and we see a bit of his relationship with Holmes and Watson. He stops in and visits with them, and they exchange information informally — Holmes gets to keep up on the latest from Scotland Yard, and Lestrade gets to ask Holmes' advice on his latest (and presumably, less interesting) cases. Lestrade continues to be a relatively good detective in his own right — obviously not as good at Holmes, but Lestrade comes to some deductions on his own. Later in the story,

Holmes is moved by Lestrade's compliment "We are not jealous of you at Scotland Yard...." In fact, Holmes actually treasures such praise quite highly:

Lestrade and I sat silent for a moment, and then, with a spontaneous impulse, we both broke out clapping as at the well-wrought crisis of a play. A flush of color sprang to Holmes' pale cheeks, and he bowed to us like the master dramatist who receives the homage of his audience. It was at such moments that for an instant he ceased to be a reasoning machine, and betrayed his human love for admiration and applause.

In attempting to date the case, there is a reference to May 20th the previous year being a payday. If we assume that May 20th is a Friday, that makes it May 20th, 1898, placing the case at 1899. However, in the story Sherlock Holmes is mentioned in one of the newspapers. But if this was after the Great Hiatus, why is Watson still kept from publishing his own accounts? Holmes just laughs at the newspaper account, so clearly he's not worried about the reference.

Since I posted this theory on my blog, my dear friend (and editor of this book) Genevieve Podleski questioned whether I could assume Friday as a payday, and she pointed me to this quote from the *Cornhill Magazine* in 1901:

...We will suppose that thirty shillings is duly entered by being brought home whole on Saturday, which is the general pay-day, though some men are paid on Friday....

That could make the payday in question May 20th, 1899, placing the case at 1900. I considered the possibility of the 1891 or 1892, but that's firmly into the Great Hiatus. So, while the year is now a little more in question, the concerns about the time frame (and thus, the appearance of Holmes in the newspaper) are still valid.

"The Six Napoleons" is a very popular story, but not one of my absolute favorites. Mainly, the story has a number of similarities to "Blue Carbuncle," and that story captured my heart earlier than this one did.

The Adventure of the Three Students (1904)

"The Three Students" is a lackluster story. In fact, the events within the story are so implausible that it actually inspired one of the very first published pieces of Sherlockian criticism, a mere few months after the story was originally printed. So that should set expectations for you.

Watson starts with another explicit obfuscation here, hiding whether Cambridge or Oxford is the setting for "our great University town." There's still a lot of debate to this day between scholars on which is which, although I learned that the clay mentioned in the story seems to be exclusive to Cambridge at the time, which is indicative. Watson seems to know Soames previously, but it's not clear how they know each other, so that doesn't add anything to the question of the university. I expect it will be one of those questions that is never fully resolved within the Sherlockian community.

We learn a bit more about Holmes' habits, specifically his frustration with being moved from his routine. When he's away from Baker Street for long periods of time, he gets cranky. He's short with his client, and insults Watson multiple times, accusing Watson of being a thug and transplanting his own bad habits onto Watson. Later, Holmes admits that he has done Watson an injustice, but throughout the case he is short and abrasive. In fact, this story is probably the best example of the "insulting Holmes" personality type that came to characterize later interpretations of the character.

Unfortunately, this story is also an example of the casual racism of the Victorian era. One of the students is named Daulat Ras, but because he is from India, he is referred to as "the Indian" throughout the story. He's also stereotyped, as in this quote:

"The second floor is inhabited by Daulat Ras, the Indian. He is a quiet, inscrutable fellow, as most of those Indians are."

There are a number of clear examples of one particular aspect of Doyle's writing style. In many of the stories, Holmes narrates his movements in a crime scene so Doyle can set the stage without interrupting the flow of the detective's deductions. It seems like a dated technique to a modern reader, but it must have been a positive boon when Holmes was adapted to various radio dramas in the early 20th century — it gave a precedent for the actors playing Holmes to similarly narrate their movements when the audience had no way of seeing what was going on. Here's a lengthy quote that shows some examples of this:

"I see. Near this little table. You can come in now. I have finished with the carpet. Let us take the little table first. Of course, what has happened is very clear. The man entered and took the papers, sheet by sheet, from the central table. He carried them over to the window table, because from there he could see if you came across the courtyard, and so could effect an escape."

"As a matter of fact he could not," said Soames, "for I entered by the side door."

"Ah, that's good! Well, anyhow, that was in his mind. Let me see the three strips. No finger impressions — no! Well, he carried over this one first and he copied it."

There are a few interesting bits about Victorian college life and how pencils are sold, but overall this story is a forgettable contribution to the canon.

The Adventure of the Golden Pince-Nez (1904)

The golden what now? A pince-nez is a style of eyeglasses popular in the 19th century. Instead of having arms that hooked around the ears, the glasses were pinched around the nose and held in place by the nose-pieces. A good iconic example of a pince-nez wearing would be Theodore Roosevelt, but the style was generally out of fashion by the 1920s or 1930s.

There's a more detailed mention of cigarettes in this story. Cigarettes are relatively novel in Victorian England at this point, but they had trouble gaining traction with the higher classes (despite the fact that Holmes smokes them in this story and Watson smokes them in *Hound* and "The Priory School"). They were seen as particularly working-class, and ended up gaining the stigma of being particularly unhealthy. Cigarettes were blamed for the various illnesses and medical problems that all tobacco products brought, because we all know that other forms of tobacco are perfectly safe, right?

At one point Professor Coram mentioned that he goes through a thousand cigarettes every fortnight. My wife used to work as a smoking cessation coach, so I asked her how much smoking that would be from a current perspective. Assuming twenty cigarettes in a modern pack of cigarettes, Coram would have to smoke just over three and a half packs a day, or nearly four cigarettes every waking hour! Granted, it seems that Mr. Smith was a smoker as well (and therefore may have smoked some of Coram's cigarettes), but that's still a hell of a lot of smoking.

Then there's the reference to Russian nihilism. The Nihilist movement started in the 1860s as an early form of anarchism, but it became known for political violence after the assassination of Tsar Alexander II in 1881. So, it's plausible that the nihilists were active in 1894, but I can't help but wonder if Doyle's portrayal of the nihilists is as accurate as his portrayals of the Mafia and the KKK were in previous stories.

Finally, there's a mysterious reference to "love-gages." I hadn't encountered the word before, and my online searching kept trying to correct the word to "gags," which ended up being less helpful and more awkward. *The New Annotated Sherlock Holmes, Vol. II* comes to the rescue. From p. 1110:

A gage is an item offered as a token or a pledge. More specifically, it used to refer to the glove offered (or thrown down) as challenge to a duel. Here, the word is used in its secondary sense, a "love-gage" being a sign of the affection one lover pledges to another.

This story opens in late November, 1894, just after the Great Hiatus. Watson's getting more specific with dating in his past few cases, and it seems the time around Holmes' return was extremely busy. We also get a quote of what is probably the densest listing of apocryphal cases I've seen so far:

As I turn over the pages I see my notes upon the repulsive story of the red leech and the terrible death of Crosby the banker. Here also I find an account of the Addleton tragedy and the singular contents of the ancient British barrow. The famous Smith-Mortimer succession case comes also within this period, and so does the tracking and arrest of Huret, the Boulevard assassin — an exploit which won for Holmes an autograph letter of thanks from the French President and the Order of the Legion of Honor.

We see detective Stanley Hopkins again, who previously showed up in "Black Peter." Watson also refers to "our pursuit of the Andaman Islander," a reference to *The Sign of the Four*. Doyle is making more and more use of his continuity as he goes on.

At one point Holmes mentions that deciphering a palimpsest (a parchment which had its writing partially or completely erased to make room for another text) was "trying work for the eyes," and some have latched on to that as an indication of Holmes' eyesight getting worse as he aged. Right now, that's the only reference I've seen to it, and without knowing how long he was staring at the palimpsest, I'm not inclined to put any weight on the idea.

I will take a moment to look back at Holmes' relationship with women, though. In the early canon his attitude towards the fairer sex was pretty clear: he would "make merry over the cleverness of women" (quoted from "A Scandal in Bohemia," naturally). Now Watson mentions that "Holmes had, when he liked, a particularly ingratiating way with women." Clearly we've seen that when he toyed with a housemaid's affections in "Charles Augustus Milverton." Far from being the emotionless machine that Watson often paints him as, Holmes would seem to have an attractiveness and charisma appealing to the opposite sex. Holmes' dismissal of women may be due to the fact that he finds them easily manipulated — Irene Adler, for example, was only taken in for a few minutes by Holmes' most elaborate ruse, while it seems that more commonplace women easily fall for his charms. He has also manipulated his own best friend, but there is no corresponding weight placed on the gullibility of men. Why the emphasis on women? Is it merely Victorian sexism, or something more?

The Adventure of the Missing Three-Quarter (1904)

Aside from a detailed look into the nuances of Victorian rugby, "The Missing Three-Quarter" is noteworthy for having another frank appraisal of Holmes' addiction. It's set circa 1896 or 1897 (based on the publication date of 1904 and the comment of it being "seven or eight years ago"), so even after the Great Hiatus Watson is still concerned about his friend's drug habit. He talks about dreading Holmes' bouts of inactivity — like all addicts, Holmes is not entirely cured, but is always one hit away from returning back to the needle. Watson's quite open about the level of his concern:

Therefore I blessed this Mr. Overton, whoever he might be, since he had come with his enigmatic message to break that dangerous calm which brought more peril to my friend than all the storms of his tempestuous life.

However, Watson has "gradually weaned him from that drug mania which had threatened once check his remarkable career." There's no indication of when this might have happened, but it is fodder for one of the more infamous Holmes pastiches in the 20th century, *The Seven-Per-Cent Solution*. Although *Solution* has to declare certain stories in the canon fabricated in order to make the premise work (and takes some decidedly strong swings at some of the stories in the later canon to boot), it's one of the first novels I read that focused on Holmes the man instead of his crime-fighting career, and it's stuck with me ever since. I highly recommend it as a pastiche in the spirit of Doyle's work, if not a strictly canonical attempt at one.

Adding to our growing collection of common Victorian ailments is a reference to "consumption," a disease we now know as tuberculosis. One fact that has stuck in my head over the years is that consumption was originally believed to be the result of vampirism. That doesn't really relate to anything particular in this story, but I've always thought that the presence of consumption in various horror novels around the mid to late 19th century was an unintentional nod to the triumph of scientific study over superstition, and I'm glad it's finally made its way into the Holmes canon here.

Speaking of the canon, there's a nice little collection of canon-watching points in this story.

- There's yet another reference to Stanley Hopkins, but he's only mentioned in passing as the one who referred the case to Holmes.
- At this point, Watson claims that he has lost touch with the medical profession, so much that he didn't recognize the name of one of the heads of the medical school for the University in which the story is set. However, we know from previous stories that he keep up to date with medical journals.
- We have another reference to Moriarty (or at least that Dr. Armstrong could fill in the gap left by Moriarty). As a twist, Dr. Armstrong turns out to be an ally rather than an enemy, but again we continue to build Moriarty's sinister reputation even after the character's demise.

- Pompey is introduced. He is a hound that fulfills much the same role as my beloved Toby from *The Sign of the Four*. However, Pompey succeeds where Toby failed. Don't judge my love for Toby.
- It is mentioned that Cambridge is an "inhospitable town," which implies that Holmes might be from Oxford. It seems unlikely, though, that Holmes would be ignorant of rugby if he went to any British University, given the popularity of the sport at that time. This reference is the grist for an entirely new set of arguments around the "which college did Holmes go to" argument.

Sadly, this is another story where Holmes doesn't really solve anything — he just follows the doctor, and stumbles across the solution. But for all that, the story is worth reading for the opening references to Holmes' addiction alone.

The Adventure of the Abbey Grange (1904)

This is another case with Stanley Hopkins. We find out that Hopkins has called Holmes in on seven cases as of 1897, but we only have four stories in which Hopkins appears.

It's also the case with the sole instance of Holmes saying "The game is afoot." Let me make that clear: this is the *only* time he says this in the entire canon (although Watson references it once more in "Wisteria Lodge"). It is hardly the catchphrase that many people believe it to be, although the fact that it *actually exists* makes it way more legitimate than "Elementary, my dear Watson." It's believed that "the game is afoot" is paraphrased from Shakespeare, either *Henry the Fourth*, Act I, Scene 3, or *Henry the Fifth*, Act III, Scene 1.

Watson's writing and publication of Holmes' cases becomes a sore spot in the story, and Watson gets a little testy about it:

Your fatal habit of looking at everything from the point of view of a story instead of as a scientific exercise has ruined what might have been an instructive and even classical series of demonstrations. You slur over work of the utmost finesse and delicacy, in order to dwell upon sensational details which may excite, but cannot possibly instruct, the reader."

"Why do you not write them yourself?" I said, with some bitterness.

"I will, my dear Watson, I will."

(Actually, Holmes does write up two cases himself later — "The Blanched Soldier" and "The Lion's Mane.")

As for Holmes himself, we learn that he is nearly six feet tall. He lists the suspect as "six foot three in height," and that he is "at least three inches a bigger man than I." Holmes is also unusually taken in by the story from Lady Brackenstall — so much that he actually leaves the scene of the case and has to reconsider it before he discounts the testimony and returns. Of course, this story was written before the style of American detective fiction was created, where clients and witnesses were assumed to be lying, but Holmes had always been fairly critical of both physical and testimonial evidence in previous cases.

Let's look at Doyle's writing a little more closely here. On the one hand, there are a couple of good instances of Doyle short-cutting through unnecessary talk. One of the better examples (where Holmes' response is omitted):

135

"I have told you all that happened, Mr. Hopkins," she said, wearily. *"Could you not repeat it for me? Well, if you think it necessary, I will tell these gentlemen what occurred."*

On the other hand, some of Lady Brackenstall's testimony sounds forced.

"But the main reason lies in the one fact, which is notorious to everyone, and that is that Sir Eustace was a confirmed drunkard. To be with such a man for an hour is unpleasant. Can you imagine what it means for a sensitive and high-spirited woman to be tied to him for day and night? It is a sacrilege, a crime, a villainy to hold that such a marriage is binding."

Who talks about themselves as a "sensitive and high-spirited woman" like that? Even given the stilted cadence of Victorian fiction, this sounds particular awkward, especially for a more polished writer like Doyle.

A couple of things about 19th century society to note. There's more casual racism in this story, specifically "I believe you are a man of your word, and a white man...." Although still appallingly racist to modern readers, it was contemporary American slang that meant "an honest man" (and has lingered on afterwards as "That's mighty white of you"). There are also a number of references to beeswing, which turns out to be the flaky deposit found in certain kinds of bottle-aged wines like port.

The Adventure of the Second Stain (1904)

Thus we come to the final story in *The Return of Sherlock Holmes*, and the last story before another gap in Doyle's tales of the Great Detective. This time Doyle doesn't try to kill Holmes off, but he's still pretty blunt — Watson details how "Abbey Grange" was supposed to be the last story, because Holmes doesn't want them published anymore since his retirement, but "The Second Stain" is really the one we end on. We do get a small glimpse into Holmes' retirement, however: study and bee-keeping in the Sussex Downs. It seems he has also come to hate his fame, which is a change of pace from the younger Holmes who craved attention.

Back in "The Naval Treaty," there was a mention about a case involving a second stain, but that reference is inconsistent with details in this story. Here's the quote from "Treaty" to compare:

The July which immediately succeeded my marriage was made memorable by three cases of interest, in which I had the privilege of being associated with Sherlock Holmes and of studying his methods. I find them recorded in my notes under the headings of "The Adventure of the Second Stain," "The Adventure of the Naval Treaty," and "The Adventure of the Tired Captain." The first of these, however, deals with interest of such importance and implicates so many of the first families in the kingdom that for many years it will be impossible to make it public. No case, however, in which Holmes was engaged has ever illustrated the value of his analytical methods so clearly or has impressed those who were associated with him so deeply. I still retain an almost verbatim report of the interview in which he demonstrated the true facts of the case to Monsieur Dubugue of the Paris police, and Fritz von Waldbaum, the well-known specialist of Dantzig, both of whom had wasted their energies upon what proved to be side-issues. The new century will have come, however, before the story can be safely told.

Since this is a case involving highly-placed public officials (similar to the "The Bruce-Partington Plans"), the timing of the case is explicitly vague. Even the decade is kept secret. Holmes and Watson live together, so we have the usual timeframes for guesses (pre-wedding or post-Hiatus). Because of a passing mention to the Prime Minister having a second term, dates on the case could range from 1886 to 1902, depending on which Prime Minister. Despite the reference above to "the July which immediately succeeded my marriage," the case is very likely one in which Watson is an unmarried man, since he spent three days without comment at 221B Baker Street. Therefore, either the reference in "Treaty" is wrong, or the details in this story are too obfuscated to slot into continuity. I'm more inclined towards assuming "Treaty" is wrong and that this case is set in the late 1890s, because Watson is just as quick as Holmes to contribute to the case when Holmes talks about the three men who might be involved:

"There are only those three capable of playing so bold a game; there are Oberstein, La Rothiere, and Eduardo Lucas. I will see each of them."

I glanced at my morning paper.

"Is that Eduardo Lucas of Godolphin Street?"

"Yes."

"You will not see him."

"Why not?"

"He was murdered in his house last night."

My friend has so often astonished me in the course of our adventures that it was with a sense of exultation that I realized how completely I had astonished him.

Later, Watson claims the murder as a wild coincidence, and Holmes chides him. However, Watson turns out to be completely correct. (Holmes, of course, gives Watson no credit for this.)

On a side note, two of the three men mentioned above are Oberstein and La Rothiere. These two were also referenced in "The Bruce-Partington Plans," and their residences in the West End were established in both stories as well. The way both stories are phrased, it's hard to tell which case comes first, but given that two highly-influential men in the British government are speaking openly to Holmes and without Mycroft present, I'm inclined to believe this case comes after "Bruce-Partington," as Holmes proved his discretion and talent in that case.

Watson's experience with women comes up again. He is clearly smitten by a beautiful woman, and Holmes chides Watson for the fair sex being his department before admitting that he finds women inscrutable.

Lestrade is back, and he is confiding in Holmes. This is another indication to me that this is a later story, as Lestrade trusts Holmes enough to admonish his own patrolman just on Holmes' word. Also, Watson refers to multiple friends of Holmes at one point, and it's possible that Lestrade might be considered a friend by this point in their relationship.

The international situation referred to in the story closely resembles the political situation of the early 20th century, and

139

unfortunately the Great War alluded to in the story actually did come about (as World War I). Further, when Holmes writes the name of the author of the provocative letter, the Premier says only "Exactly. It was he." It's commonly believed by Sherlockians that the allusion is to Kaiser Wilhelm II, the emperor of Germany and the king of Prussia, because of Wilhelm's legendary lack of political tact.

Finally, another little snippet of Victorian lexicon. Lestrade says in the story "I've lucky for you, my man, that nothing is missing, or you would find yourself in Queer Street." According to the *Dictionary of Phrase and Fable* (1898), to live in Queer Street means to be of doubtful solvency or to be marked as someone worthy of questioning. While the use of "queer" to mean homosexual ranged back as early as 1894, it wasn't a universal meaning, and queer was still used in the early 1900s to refer to an irregularity or something counterfeit.

Although there's not a lot of development of Holmes or Watson in this story, it's actually quite a good classic tale and an interesting twist on an espionage story. Holmes is in classic form, Watson has a couple of good moments, and the relationship between Holmes and Lestrade is mature. This is one of my favorites.

The Valley of Fear (1914-1915)

The final novel, and throughout the story we get quite a conflicted picture of Holmes. For example, near the start of the book Holmes explicitly calls out Watson, saying "You are developing a certain unexpected vein of pawky humor, Watson, against which I must learn to guard myself." However, Holmes is certainly not above his own sense of "pawky humor," like when he says "Perhaps there are points which have escaped your Machiavellian intellect." Further, Watson says that Holmes is warmed by genuine admiration, and Holmes even admits to being dramatic:

> Holmes laughed. "Watson insists that I am the dramatist in real life," said he. "Some touch of the artist wells up within me, and calls insistently for a well-staged performance. Surely our profession, Mr. Mac, would be a drab and sordid one if we did not sometimes set the scene so as to glorify our results. The blunt accusation, the brutal tap upon the shoulder—what can one make of such a denouement? But the quick inference, the subtle trap, the clever forecast of coming events, the triumphant vindication of bold theories—are these not the pride and the justification of our life's work? At the present moment you thrill with the glamour of the situation and the anticipation of the hunt. Where would be that thrill if I had been as definite as a timetable?"

But despite that, Holmes is also the emotionless, calculating detective, as Watson likens his reception of horrific news to a "chemist who sees the crystals falling into position from his oversaturated solution." Holmes also reiterates his negative stance on women ("I am not a whole-souled admirer of womankind, as you are aware...") and seems uncomfortable with

Watson's bluntness ("There is an appalling directness about your questions, Watson...").

None of these facts come across as directly contradictory, but in the space of the novel we have more opportunities to see Holmes, and we can appreciate what a complicated and nuanced personality he has. Here is a man that is harsh with his criticism and yet craves admiration, one who fights fiercely with his best friend one moment and gently jokes with him the next. He can speak eloquently on the beauty of a particular mystery as easily as he can read one of the many ciphers he uses to amuse his intelligence. He is a temperamental artist inside the shell of a soulless scientist, and yet neither extreme would make him the masterful detective that he is. This is Holmes in his prime.

(Also, apparently Holmes' eyebrows are "bushy," although it's only mentioned in this novel.)

Watson, while he doesn't have nearly as large a part as he did in *Hound*, still manages to reinforce his character and provide some new elements. His humility crops up, causing him at one point to ask leave to remove his "own insignificant personality" from the narrative. Further, though Holmes chides Watson about his knowledge of women, Watson cools quite quickly to the beautiful Mrs. Parker when he believes her to be part of the conspiracy. He doesn't love women any less, but he's not as easily swayed by them as he was in the earlier cases.

Holmes' relationship with the police is very different than in previous stories, or at least less fractious. Holmes' fame has spread to the point that even the provincial police force in Sussex knows of Sherlock Holmes, even though depending on the timing of the case (which I'll get into more, below — I wouldn't miss an opportunity to bitch about chronology!) Holmes would barely be known. Admittedly, White Mason is a friend of MacDonald, and MacDonald is very keen on Holmes, so it's possible that MacDonald mentioned Holmes to Mason in passing before. However, the positive esteem that the official officers hold Holmes in (and the positive impression that both men make on Holmes) is very different from the love/hate relationship that Lestrade has with Holmes. Further, MacDonald and Mason are both quite bright. Holmes brings up points during Mason's deconstruction of the possible events, and Mason takes them in stride. Clearly, he's keeping up with Holmes. It really brings home the fact that, as we go deeper into the later canon, the official detectives are just as often intelligent men that Holmes respects as they are ignorant men that he rails against.

The Valley of Fear actually involves Moriarty a fair amount, although he never appears in the book — if "The Final Problem" is the best source for learning about how Moriarty is as a man, this book is the best for bits about Moriarty's organization and the people around him. We learn that he pays his men well, and for their intelligence ("the American business principle"). He is a very firm leader, and any violation of his word results in death. He has an agent named Porlock that either betrays him or pretends to betray him to lure Holmes out — different Sherlockians have argued different interpretations on that, as well as offering a variety of opinions on who "Fred Porlock" really is.

We also learn another piece about Moriarty's family. In "The Final Problem," Watson mentions that Professor Moriarty's death is defended by his older brother, Colonel James Moriarty. In this story, it is mentioned that his *younger* brother is a station-master in the west of England. Does Moriarty have two brothers? (Kim Newman's wonderful parody *The Hound of the D'Urbervilles* takes exactly this approach in the story "The Greek Invertebrate," to hilarious effect.)

There is a big problem with all this Moriarty business, though. "The Final Problem" makes very clear that Watson had not known of Moriarty before that case, and Holmes was equally clear that very few people knew of him or his deeds. However, both of these facts are contradicted here: Watson clearly hears of Moriarty in this case (which has to be before "The Final Solution"), and MacDonald also knows about Moriarty. Trying to date this case after "Problem" isn't any easier — why isn't anyone concerned that Moriarty isn't dead, or that Moran isn't in jail after his arrest in "The Empty House"?

The text doesn't help the task of dating the case any. The most obvious method is to take the explicit year reference in the second half of the book (1875), and combine it with that section's reference of "I wish you to journey back some twenty years in time...." 1875 plus twenty years leads to the case being in 1895, which is after the Great Hiatus. Watson (typically, at this point) doesn't mention his wife, so it could be after his "tragedy" in 1894. But when Holmes meets up with MacDonald, there's a reference to "the early days at the end of the '80's," which puts it before the Great Hiatus. Madness!

There is simply no way to reconcile the facts presented in this book without ignoring some of them. I am more inclined to discount the second half of the book (for many reasons), stick with the bulk of the evidence in the first half, which points towards a case around 1887 or so, and pretend that Watson created the effect of asking about Moriarty in "The Final Problem" as a narrative device rather than a literal conversation that happened in 1891. At least Holmes' deduction of what book to use for the cipher (another good example of object-based deduction) tells us that the case starts on January 7th (which, for reasons I've never been entirely clear on, some Sherlockians believe proves that January 7th is Holmes' birthday).

Speaking of MacDonald, Holmes' relationship with the two police characters is quite interesting. We're told that Inspector MacDonald is rather famous, although we never hear of him before or after this case. He has, by the time of this story, consulted Holmes twice in the past. Holmes refers familiarly to MacDonald as "Mr. Mac" multiple times, while Lestrade and other detectives are only referred to with courtesy and their full title.

It's a bit easy to cast that aside as a fluke, perhaps, but the respect that Holmes shows both men is displayed over and over again. Once, the two policemen quickly accept Holmes' theories and discard their own almost immediately — no stubborn Lestrade trying to cram his own theories down Holmes' throat. In return, Holmes mentions explicitly that he would "play fairly" with them, and he offers to hand the case over to the official men as soon as possible:

"I only wish to verify my details in one way, which can very readily be done, and then I make my bow and return to London, leaving my results entirely at your service. I owe you too much to act otherwise...."

Where's the personal justice? Where are the snide comments about the efficiency of the official force? MacDonald is clearly a favorite of Holmes, but the relationship is way too pat, too bland in this story. It's possible (as was pointed out to me when I first wrote this essay) that Doyle realized that the Metropolitan Police were made up of people with feelings, and Doyle's wide-flung fame had painted them in a very negative light — thus creating a new detective (rather than trying to redeem Gregson or Lestrade) and presenting them in a more positive and productive light. To this, I say "bah." Give me Lestrade's stubborn bungling over this milquetoast efficiency any day.

Really, this book just continually frustrates me. That is likely due in part to the fact that *The Valley of Fear* is set up almost identically to *A Study in Scarlet*. From half of the book being set in a different time and written by a different narrator down to the use of another American secret society and even a key clue revolving around a wedding ring, this book feels like a rewrite. Even the gimmick of weighing down evidence with heavy objects comes from "The Man with the Twisted Lip"!

But irritating similarities aside, Doyle has some good bits here. There's a classic locked-room mystery that's probably one of the best in the canon, and most of the investigation feels more like modern mystery writing — revolving around a number of testimonies, and trying to sort out which are the lies and how to deduce the truth from the falsehoods. It's actually got a hard-boiled feel. The second half of the novel, despite having little to do with Holmes, is still a fun pulp-style story of an undercover Pinkerton that would be great to read in another book. Doyle takes a stab at writing some accents (although he only seems to focus on Scottish and German). At one point, Doyle actually takes a poke at himself and the growing detective fiction field through MacDonald:

"I don't take much stock of detectives in novels—chaps that do things and never let you see how they do them. That's just inspiration: not business."

Finally, there are some interesting Victorian details in this story. During the cipher deduction, we learn that almanacs are quite common books to have in most Victorian homes. We see more bicycles, and MacDonald mentions the idea of giving them license plates. The American secret society this time is a thinly-veiled combination of the Molly Maguires and the Ancient Order of Hibernians (a fraternal organization of Irish Catholics). Also, Watson mentions "peine forte et dure," which was a method of torture used by the French legal system. In peine forte et dure, a defendant who refuses to plead had subsequently larger and heavier stones put on his chest until he stopped breathing or entered a plea. The longer stories are great for this kind of Victorian detail, which I love.

So, this book sits in the same place as *A Study in Scarlet* for me. What it lacks in the canon-establishing detail, it makes up for it with a few bright spots of writing and some great Victorian flavor. The second half of the book is still easily skipped from the perspective of the canon, and Doyle seems to get fed up with his own writing at points, but it's has its (rare) bright moments.

His Last Bow

The Adventure of Wisteria Lodge (1908)

"Wisteria Lodge" is an odd story in the canon. It honestly reads as if someone else besides Doyle wrote it, ham-fistedly emulating some parts of Doyle's style while explicitly ignoring others. The simplest example of this shows up right out of the gate, with the story being set in March 1892, although this is during the Great Hiatus!

The larger and more insidious deviation from the Holmes formula is Inspector Baynes. Even though Inspector Gregson (from *Scarlet* and "The Greek Interpreter") is mentioned, we meet a new Inspector, who right away makes a thoroughly detailed examination of a note that is a pitch-perfect emulation of Holmes' own methods. He compliments Holmes, who is pleased by the flattery, but Baynes plays his cards close to his chest, exactly as Holmes does. In fact, Baynes appears to make an error, arresting the wrong person, before revealing that it was a ruse to lure out the real criminal. In essence, at every point Baynes out-detects Holmes, and yet Holmes seems impressed rather than irritated with this official policeman. This is the only time in the official canon that we see this kind of competent policeman, which makes the strange near-parody of Holmes stand out in the canon all that much more.

However, some of the classic touches we expect from a Holmes story by this point are here. For example, Watson makes a reference to "the game is afoot," and makes two explicit mentions of past cases ("The Red-Headed League" and "The Five Orange Pips"). Holmes even insults Watson's stories twice:

"If you cast your mind back to some of those narratives with which you have afflicted a long-suffering public..."

As well as:

"You are like my friend, Dr. Watson, who has a bad habit of telling his stories wrong end foremost."

There's also a stray reference to an apocryphal case — "we locked up Colonel Carruthers." Actually, this reference brings to mind something I hadn't noticed before: there are an awfully large number of criminal Colonels in the canon:

- Colonel Barclay ("The Crooked Man")
- Colonel Dorking ("Charles Augustus Milverton")
- Colonel Emsworth ("The Blanched Soldier")
- Colonel Openshaw ("The Five Orange Pips")
- Colonel Stark ("The Engineer's Thumb")
- Colonel Upwood (*Hound of the Baskervilles*)
- Colonel Walter ("The Bruce-Partington Plans")
- Colonel Warburton ("The Engineer's Thumb")
- And, of course, Colonel Moran ("The Empty House")

There is a passing reference to voodoo, perhaps the earliest literary reference to it, but it's not enough to redeem this story.

The Adventure of the Cardboard Box (1892)

"The Cardboard Box" is actually a good classic tale, if a bit darker than some others in the canon. Of course, part of the reason why it feels more classic in tone is that it was published a good fifteen years before the previous story. The story was considered so controversial that Arthur Conan Doyle suppressed publication of the story in the first edition of *Memoirs*, and American publishers didn't reprint it until *His Last Bow*. In my cursory research, I couldn't find any information on why he suppressed the story — it appears none of his biographies address the point. Mysterious....

Anyhow, since this was published in 1892 (and thus, before "The Final Problem"), the story is clearly set pre-Hiatus. However, *The Sign of the Four* is mentioned, so it has to be post-marriage, but his wife is never mentioned, and it is implied (although not stated out-right) that Watson is living with Holmes. It is possible that it took place in the increasingly cramped space between Watson's engagement and his marriage, though.

Regardless, this story is full of great little details. We learn that Watson is good at tolerating heat better than the cold, due to his wartime activities. There is a reference to Watson's wound ("Your hand stole towards your own old wound"), but no clarity on the "leg or shoulder" debate. We discover that Holmes does not like to go out for the holidays, preferring to stay in the city and that "[a]ppreciation of nature found no place among his many gifts." Holmes' violin obsession comes out here, including his detailed knowledge of Paganini and the often-noted reference to his owning a Stradivarius violin. We learn that Holmes has written "two short monographs" about the ear in the *Anthropological Journal*.

More interestingly (and perhaps, more tellingly), Watson casually mentions a "depleted bank account." I was reminded of a similar reference in "The Dancing Men," where Holmes reminds Watson that his checkbook was locked up in Holmes' drawer. Some have drawn a connection between these two quotes, and a few have even connected both with Watson's familiarity with horse races and gambling, painting the picture of a man who is perhaps more free with his money than he should be.

But the scene that gets the most attention is the one right near the front. In it, Sherlock deduces Watson's thought processes by observing his actions. The first and most commonly cited problem with this section is that it's completely reprinted in the American version of "The Resident Patient." Word for word, the whole scene is duplicated there — likely because the American editors liked the scene even though they didn't like "The Cardboard Box," so they edited it (rather clumsily) into "The Resident Patient." But more than that, and more frustrating to me, is the complete reversal that Holmes has. First, there's this quote from "Cardboard Box":

"You remember," said he, "that some little time ago when I read you the passage in one of Poe's sketches in which a close reasoner follows the unspoken thoughts of his companion, you were inclined to treat the matter as a mere tour-de-force of the author. On my remarking that I was constantly in the habit of doing the same thing you expressed incredulity."

Now, compare it to this quote from *A Study in Scarlet*:

Sherlock Holmes rose and lit his pipe. "No doubt you think that you are complimenting me in comparing me to Dupin," he observed. "Now, in my opinion, Dupin was a very inferior fellow. That trick of his of breaking in on his friends' thoughts with an apropos remark after a quarter of an hour's silence is really very showy and superficial. He had some analytical genius, no doubt; but he was by no means such a phenomenon as Poe appeared to imagine."

Quite showy and superficial? *You're doing the same thing, Holmes.* Not only is Holmes contradicting himself, but he's shoving his own dismissal of Dupin onto Watson! I could say that this is actually intentional and a foible of Holmes' (and there are some places in the canon that implies that Holmes does exactly that), but I suspect that this is a flat-out contradiction. Some people rage about the character change that results from having Greedo shoot Han Solo first in the original *Star Wars*, and to me this is on par with that. If we accept that it's intentional, it means that Holmes has somehow come to believe that Dupin is now on Holmes' level, and is attempting to shove it under the rug by pretending that Watson was the skeptical one. But this same story shows how egotistical Holmes really is.

> *"I should prefer that you do not mention my name at all in connection with the case, as I choose to be only associated with those crimes which present some difficulty in their solution."*

Lestrade agrees that it is simple, and Holmes is bothered by that, reinforcing his egotism. Further, the whole deductive scene at the start really paints Watson as a bit of a buffoon. I actually hope that it's a mistake, because I would rather have a contradiction in the canon than think of Holmes — thus far proving to be egotistical and full of confidence in his own abilities — as being willing to insult and offend his friend in order to validate a foreign detective.

That ranting aside, there are some great little Victorian details here. Our old friend, brain fever, makes another appearance. Holmes mentions driving to a decent hotel in order to have lunch — apparently hotels served lunch to people who weren't staying there. There's also mention of blue ribbons, a reference to a temperance organization. The use of blue ribbons by contemporary temperance organizations is believed to come from Numbers 15:38:

Speak unto the children of Israel, and bid them that they make them fringes in the borders of their garments, throughout their generations, and that they put upon the fringe of the borders a ribband of blue....

Finally, one of the theories through the story is that the delivery of the severed ears are a prank from some medical students. This reminds me of the notorious actions of the "resurrectionists," or the grave robbers of the day. Medical schools of the time could only dissect the bodies of condemned criminals, but early in the 1800s the practice had dropped off, and there came to be an illegal trade in corpses. Two of the most notorious grave robbers were William Burke and William Hare, who actually turned to murder in order to provide the number of corpses necessary. Their actions ultimately led to the passing of the Anatomy Act of 1832, which expanded the number of corpses available for medical dissection. If you're interested, Robert Louis Stevenson's short story "The Body Snatcher" was based on the exploits of Burke and Hare.

The Adventure of the Red Circle (1911)

After "The Cardboard Box," we jump eighteen years ahead to "The Red Circle." Holmes starts right off by being insulting to a landlady, and goes on to mock the agony columns of the newspapers he reads (in what has become one of my favorite bits of Holmes ranting about something):

"Dear me!" said he, turning over the pages, "what a chorus of groans, cries, and bleatings! What a rag-bag of singular

*happenings! ...'Every day my heart longs —' Bleat, Watson —
unmitigated bleat!"*

To clarify, the agony columns are not what we think of them today. Nowadays an agony column is an advice column, often given by an anonymous or pseudonymous person. The agony columns Holmes talks about here were a collection of advertisements and personal messages. They were very much like a Victorian Craigslist, which certainly has had its share of bleating today. I expect Holmes would find some nuggets of interest (and quite a lot to mock) from our modern equivalents on the Internet.

There's also a longer quote that really sums up why Holmes takes some cases for little or no fee, explaining things through his scientific bent:

"Why should you go further in it? What have you to gain from it?"

"What, indeed? It is art for art's sake, Watson. I suppose when you doctored you found yourself studying cases without thought of a fee?"

"For my education, Holmes."

"Education never ends, Watson. It is a series of lessons with the greatest for the last. This is an instructive case. There is neither money nor credit in it, and yet one would wish to tidy it up."

As for other characters, we see the last appearance of Gregson, and we learn that Watson is starting to develop Holmes' biases in regards to the local police, claiming that they "may blunder in the matter of intelligence, but never in that of courage."

154

On the other hand, we find the only other reference to the Pinkertons in the canon here (aside from *The Valley of Fear*), and the only time that Holmes works directly with them. His respect for them over the local police is striking, though. Is it because Allan Pinkerton was Scottish like Doyle?

Of more historical interest, though, are the Italian references in this story. Aside from "The Six Napoleons," this is the only other canonical story to really go into the Italian culture in London at the time. First, the story claims that the fictional secret society mentioned (the titular "Red Circle") is an offshoot of another group called the Carbonari. The Carbonari were a secret political society active in the early 1800s in southern Italy. They generally believed in Italian unification and some form of constitutional government, and had their own ritual gestures, ceremonies, and other trappings (likely inspired by or stolen from Freemasonry). The Carbonari were sometimes involved in violent uprising and assassination attempts in the early 19th century, but they weren't nearly as bloody as is implied in this story. So who were the "Red Circle"?

Most of the Sherlockian scholarship I found seems to believe that the "Carbonari" is actually a reference to the Camorra, a criminal organization based around Naples. A gross over-simplification is that the Camorra are to Naples what the Mafia are to Sicily. I tend to agree with this assessment, not only because the organization names are so similar, but because the original manuscript for the story contained a reference to the Black Hand that was crossed out and replaced with Red Circle, and both the Camorra and the Mafia were erroneously called "The Black Hand Society" in the American press of the time. ("Black

155

Hand" is actually a form of heavy-handed extortion that both organizations practiced, which fell out of practice in the 1920s.)

Like many of Doyle's later stories, this one falls more on the side of "adventure story" than "mystery," but it's still fun.

The Adventure of the Bruce-Partington Plans (1908)

We continue with the strange organization of *His Last Bow* by going back to a story published three years previous to "The Red Circle," and perhaps one of the best stories in the canon — "The Bruce-Partington Plans." This story has everything: iconic images of Holmes and London, a further peek and evolution into established parts of the canon, a great case with Holmes being clever (but not too clever), and some fantastic writing by Doyle. In fact, this story is so entrenched in the canon that I sometimes confuse it with another story about espionage, "The Naval Treaty," thinking that the revelations about Mycroft appear there instead of here.

In fact, let's start with Mycroft. Holmes gives his well-known statement that Mycroft *is* the British government at times, and proceeds to explain his unique position (which, in modern times, sounds an awful lot like he's a relational database in a computer system). There's rather a lengthy quote about Mycroft in the story, but it really does cover what a unique man he is:

"He has the tidiest and most orderly brain, with the greatest capacity for storing facts, of any man living. The same great powers which I have turned to the detection of crime he has used for this particular business. The conclusions of every department are passed to him, and he is the central exchange, the

clearing-house, which makes out the balance. All other men are specialists, but his specialism is omniscience. We will suppose that a minister needs information as to a point which involves the Navy, India, Canada and the bimetallic question; he could get his separate advices from various departments upon each, but only Mycroft can focus them all, and say offhand how each factor would affect the other. They began by using him as a short-cut, a convenience; now he has made himself an essential."

As for iconic Holmes moments, this story has loads of them. It starts with four days of dense yellow fog — the fog-covered streets of London are a common image associated with Sherlock Holmes, but like his deerstalker hat, it's not one that actually appears all that often, this being one of the few times that it does. We have a scene of Holmes complaining about how dull the London criminal is, and his stance that "[i]t is fortunate for this community that I am not a criminal." He gets frustrated with how slow people around him appear to be, and he ignores a chance at high honors just for the thrill of the puzzle and the chase ("I play the game for the game's own sake..."). He writes a monograph about the music of the Middle Ages, focusing on the polyphonic motets of Lassus. He even quotes his famous maxim about eliminating the impossible and the remaining improbabilities being the truth.

We have another mention of the mysteriously nameless maid at 221B. Lestrade has a part in this story, and the description of his lean, nervous form next to Mycroft's ponderous inertia is strikingly opposite. This case is set in 1895, and we see a measure of the fame Holmes has gained — Watson mentions that Holmes was received with the respect "which my companions' card always commanded." Hugo Oberstein is mentioned again after his appearance in "The Adventure of the Second Stain." Interesting, he's one of the few minor characters in the canon who is mentioned casually in one story, only to come back with a stronger role in a later one, but he is not widely considered to be part of the minor collection of characters with the like of Lestrade or Mrs. Hudson.

Historically, the submarine plans at the heart of the story were actually a great military innovation at the time. There was an race towards a usable submarine in the late 1800s, but the first viable submarine did not come about until Germany's U-1 in 1905, fully ten years after the time this story is set in (but three years before it was published).

"The Bruce-Partington Plans" is considered by some to be an early precursor to the spy thriller, not yet developed into a genre in its own right. However, it is one of the best Holmes stories, and possibly one of the best mystery stories ever.

The Adventure of the Dying Detective (1913)

This story is one in which Holmes is incredibly cruel to Watson — not nearly as cruel as allowing Watson to believe him dead for three years, but certainly on par with it. In fact, considering that the story is set in the second year of Watson's married life (so either 1889 or 1890, depending on what year you believed Watson was married in), this smaller betrayal certainly echoes his larger one in 1891.

But Holmes' cruelty doesn't extend just to making his friend believe that he is dying. During the story, he is downright brutal with Watson, making withering comments like "if you had shared my secret you would never have been able to impress Smith with the urgent necessity of his presence" and that "you are only a general practitioner with very limited experience and mediocre qualifications" (although admittedly, Holmes later softens the blow on Watson's medical qualifications, saying "Do you imagine that I have no respect for your medical talents?"). The fact that Watson did not recognize two rare tropical diseases is hardly a reason to doubt his medical talents — Holmes himself later claims that he has to go to a specialist in the exact same kinds of disease!

Even Mrs. Hudson isn't spared Holmes' cruelty, as she is not only duped, but treated abysmally by her long-time tenant. This is one of the few stories where Mrs. Hudson gets any sort of characterization, which is fantastic, but unfortunately for her that characterization is to cement her place in the canon as "long-suffering" at the hands of Holmes.

And at the end, Holmes can do nothing but congratulate himself:

"That pretense I have carried out with the thoroughness of the true artist."

From a canonical perspective, we're introduced to Inspector Morton, who Watson claims as an "old acquaintance," even though this is the only time in the canon he is mentioned — however, some Sherlockians posit that Morton may be the unidentified partner to Inspector Brown in *The Sign of Four*. As far as historical references go, we see another example of the casual racism of the time, this time by the twice-mentioned "coolies," referring to an unskilled laborer in Asia but which later evolved into a racial slur against all "ignorant" Asians. These kinds of unskilled laborers were common in the United States as well as England at the time, particularly on the westward expansion of the railroads in the late 19th century. Their presence ultimately led to the creation of many of the West Coast Chinatowns we have in the U.S. today.

The case itself is fairly non-existent and the treatment of Watson and Mrs. Hudson is terrible, but this story is great as an example of not only the unusual relationship between the two men, but also of just how complex of a man Holmes himself is.

The Disappearance of Lady Frances Carfax (1911)

"Lady Frances Carfax" appears to be another typical story — more of Holmes deducing something from a trifling of Watson's (in this case, a Turkish bath from his boots), as well as some passing references to Lestrade and Holmes' "own small but very efficient organization," for example — but it shows what seems like a common trend in the late canon: Holmes being unfairly critical of Watson.

Similar to stories like *Hound of the Baskervilles*, Watson is sent off alone to investigate a case. Watson, to his credit, does a fine job not only picking up the trail, but beating Green to the end of the trail (and actually not informing the criminals at all — Green does a worse job of that!) However, Holmes claims Watson has made "a very pretty hash" of the investigation:

"And a singularly consistent investigation you have made, my dear Watson," said he. "I cannot at the moment recall any possible blunder which you have omitted. The total effect of your proceeding has been to give the alarm everywhere and yet to discover nothing."

Admittedly, Watson does make a single, noticeable error. At one point, Holmes asks for a description of Dr. Shlessinger's left ear. Watson, despite knowing of Holmes' methods and interest in trifles, assumes that Holmes is joking. Granted, this kind of inquiry does seem in line with Holmes' mischievous nature, and certainly the "half-humorous commendation" he received earlier might have made Watson a little defensive. Still, it's a strange fumble for Watson. Further, if Holmes is unfairly critical of Watson (one mistake is not a complete failure), he is at least correctly critical of his own performance in the case, and shows unusual respect to the criminals ("If our ex-missionary friends escape the clutches of Lestrade, I shall expect to hear of some brilliant incidents in their future career").

Aside from Watson's performance as a detective, this is certainly a case later in their collective careers, and Watson mentions feeling old. That reference has caused many scholars (as well as myself) to place this case sometime after 1900, although there is no consensus on a specific year. Further, the Hotel National wasn't listed in *Baedeker's Switzerland Guide* until 1902, which seems to confirm that dating.

Holmes dislikes leaving the country because "Scotland Yard feels lonely without me, and it causes an unhealthy excitement among the criminal classes," although his appearance later in the story seems to put the lie to that particular claim, as well as his lengthy time abroad during the Great Hiatus.

There are a number of interesting historical details nestled through the text. Not having a servant at a certain class of society is considered to be suspicious. Medical science at the time had two methods for resuscitation: artificial respiration and injected ether. Being buried alive was a very real Victorian fear, to the point where some coffins installed bells and other devices to allow any inhabitant to indicate that they were still alive. Turkish baths were considered to be a medical "alterative" (not "alternative," as some texts try to assert) or treatment used to alter the course of an illness. But most prominent is the discussion of the habits (both social and financial) of single high-class ladies. For example, Holmes points out that "Single ladies must live, and their passbooks are compressed diaries." We also learn that some lonely ladies found comfort and occupation in religion, and that they are sometimes the instigator or inspiration for crime, although those points may be Holmes' sexism rather than objective truisms.

"Carfax" is interesting for the context and information it provides, even if the story it ultimately tells is only passingly fair.

The Adventure of the Devil's Foot (1917)

Like *Hound of the Baskervilles* and the upcoming "Sussex Vampire," this is a case in which a supernatural explanation is presented, but Holmes ends up explaining the case in a very mundane fashion. More than that, it has a great example of the depth of Holmes' and Watson's friendship, one of the best quotes from Holmes, and a peek into Holmes' love life (or, more accurately, the lack of one).

In fact, let's dive into that. Holmes says, quite plainly, "I have never loved, Watson," and not too far after Holmes had (perhaps needlessly) endangered his friend's life. This is one of those scenes that have encouraged many fans to believe that there is something more than friendship between Holmes and Watson. I do agree at least that his comment is likely hyperbolic — whether you point to Watson's friendship as love or his more plausible (if still unusual) love for Irene Adler, Holmes has in all likelihood felt love — but I think extrapolating that the two had a homosexual relationship is a bit much. It's certainly an intriguing pastiche idea, and there have even been anthologies around the topic (such as *A Study in Lavender*), but there isn't any significant evidence that it's canonical. On the other hand, Watson alludes to something sinister when he says of Holmes' condition that it was "aggravated, perhaps, by occasional indiscretions of his own." We don't learn any more, but most Sherlockians consider this to be a reference to his drug habit rather than any kind of sexual indiscretions, especially since this is the second case (after "Reigate Squires") in which Holmes has worked himself into a state of illness. Holmes is the original workaholic.

Naturally, Holmes is not going to just sit still and recover, and Watson is upset at the intrusion into Holmes' recovery. He specifically mentioned that Holmes "sat up in his chair like an old hound who hears the view-halloa," which is a fox-hunting reference to the sound a dog makes when it spots the fox — a singularly appropriate metaphor for Holmes. And later in the story, Watson again compares Holmes to a hunter on the heels of his quarry. Certainly there have been a number of analogies of Holmes' methods being like a hunt (such as his most famous "The game is afoot"), but in this story the analogy is quite distinct.

Watson mentions Holmes' aversion to publicity. This is certainly borne out in aspects such as his willingness to give credit to the official forces in the newspapers, and this explanation is what's given for Doyle's slowdown of producing more stories. And again, Doyle pretends that the events of the case are actually related to (fictional) sensational news years back, this time to the "Cornish Horror." This is different from writers who try to insert Holmes into actual historical events such as pursuing Jack the Ripper. Instead, Doyle invents a story and then claims that everyone has heard about it and knows about it. The end result is the same — it gives the story the feeling of authenticity, and it certainly helped convince a number of readers that Sherlock Holmes was real.

We find out that Watson is learning Holmes' methods quite well, as he is amused when others are surprised by Holmes' "simple deduction." We also learn that Holmes "has never been known to write when a telegram would serve," reasserting this love of technology. We find out (or perhaps more accurately, Watson spells out what we already know) that Holmes has a "half-humorous, half-cynical vein which was his habitual attitude to those about him." We have another case in which Holmes enacts his own justice, deciding to let a murderer go free.

But there are two big elements in this story that are worth looking at: the conflict between the supernatural and the logical, and probably one of the most memorable scenes of friendship between the two principal characters. On the supernatural vs. the logical, it is telling that while Victorian characters such as the vicar immediately leap to supernatural conclusions, they come to someone who is logical in approach for answers. There's an interesting balance in the Victorian psyche between the exultation of reason and the lingering superstition of the age. By the early 20th century there was the rise of a variety of Sherlock Holmes imitators, including the so-called "psychic detectives" that attempted to bridge such a divide by providing logical, deductive reasoning to supernatural occurrences. One of the more famous examples is Thomas Carnacki (created by William Hope Hodgson), but there are also characters such as Flaxman Low, Jules de Grandin, Dr. John Silence, and others. Indeed, there's a whole subgenre of late Victorian to early Edwardian occult detectives, and if you're interested, you can find some gems with a few strategic searches around public domain ebook sites.

Before I get into the iconic scene of the self-poisoning of Holmes and Watson, though, I have to rant for a bit. In the scene, Holmes, after carefully explaining that the poison is activated by combustion, proceeds to light it. He does ask if Watson is actually sensible and wants to have no part in it, but it appears that Watson declines. Why in the hell would they do this? Scholars have pointed to the scene way back in *A Study in Scarlet* where it's mentioned that Holmes would be just as likely to experiment on his friends, but there has to be plenty of other, safer methods to test this poison. Further, why is Holmes surprised that it was so sudden of a transformation? He himself mentioned that the sister and two brothers were taken very soon after Mortimer Tregennis left. At least Holmes is suitable abashed, and Watson is (as ever) tolerant and loyal.

But the images that Watson sees under the influence of the poison resonate more with horror writers like Edgar Allen Poe and (later) H. P. Lovecraft, rather than the usual adventure or mystery fare. The connection to Poe, at least, is probably intentional — the element of a combustible poison is also a part of Poe's story "The Imp of the Perverse," written in 1845. This connection between Holmes and horror isn't lost on pastiche writers, as there have been a number of stories connecting Holmes and Watson with Gothic horror, including the sometimes-amazing anthology *Shadows over Baker Street*. (I particularly recommend Neil Gaiman's "A Study in Emerald," by the way.)

Regardless, it all leads to this brief, but very touching moment:

"Upon my word, Watson!" said Holmes at last with an unsteady voice, "I owe you both my thanks and an apology. It was an unjustifiable experiment even for one's self, and doubly so for a friend. I am really very sorry."

"You know," I answered with some emotion, for I have never seen so much of Holmes' heart before, "that it is my greatest joy and privilege to help you."

Finally, we have another fantastic case of Holmes' wit — one often quoted by Sherlockians, but not usually heard outside of that circle, sadly:

"How do you know that?"

"I followed you."

"I saw no one."

"That is what you may expect to see when I follow you."

His Last Bow (1917)

We come to Doyle's second attempt to put Holmes behind him — "His Last Bow." This story is one of the most unusual in the canon — it doesn't feature Holmes or Watson all that much, it's the first story written entirely in the third person (leading many Sherlockians to theorize on which character actually wrote it — I personally lean towards Mycroft), it's the last recorded case in the official canon (taking place eleven years after "The Creeping Man," even though that story hasn't been written yet), and overall it's really more of a pulp adventure than a mystery.

Some publications listed the subtitle of "His Last Bow" as "An Epilogue of Sherlock Holmes," but the version I read listed it as "The War Service of Sherlock Holmes," which is more appropriate to me — this story is absolutely about World War I. Much of the exposition of the story centers on the politics of the war at the time. Doyle mentions that August 4, 1914 is "the most terrible August in the history of the world" because this is when England declared war on Germany, followed shortly by other declarations of war between various countries — in other words, the de facto start of the Great War.

There's also some unexpected insight into the thoughts of the Irish-Americans towards England at the time. It turns out that Germany was sympathetic to the anti-British sentiment after the question of Home Rule failed to pass with the declaration of war, and they supplied arms to two of the insurgent militia forces, one of which was the precursor to the IRA. Therefore, an Irish-American working for a German spy isn't that implausible. Doyle had been heavily involved in "the Irish question" all his life (he was staunchly anti-Home Rule, a point on which he constantly disagreed with his mother), and his interests shine through clearly here.

Due to the time frame, this is the only Holmes story that is explicitly post-Edwardian, and as such there are a lot of fascinating little details we don't otherwise see in the rest of the canon. Holmes is retired, but the Prime Minister was able to convince him to leave retirement, and on an assignment of impressive scale — Holmes spends two years finding this German spy ring, and uses tactics very similar to those used by Birdy Edwards in *The Valley of Fear* to infiltrate it. There's a reference to Holmes' retirement occupation of bee-keeping in the package that Holmes gives to the German spy (a book that Holmes wrote on the topic). Holmes mentions working with Irene Adler, and that he is known in Germany. But the characters are still very much their Victorian selves — even though the fashion had changed to where friends referred to each other by first name, Holmes and Watson still refer to each other by their surnames. Holmes still values skill over morality in comments like "it is better than to fall before some more ignoble foe." And Watson is very much his old self, as Holmes himself notes: "Good old Watson! You are the one fixed point in a changing age."

There are lots of historical details as well, including a reference to the "Marconi wireless" which would eventually become the radio. More interesting to modern pulp fans, perhaps, is a reference to Zeppelin — not only the airship, but the inventor. Count Ferdinand von Zeppelin was a retired German military office who invented a motor-driven airship called LZ-1 in 1900. By the end of WWI, the German military used over a hundred Zeppelins, and that proliferation of airships is mentioned in this story.

As a spy story it's not great, with a spymaster who is singularly incompetent and with Holmes acting more out of panache than secrecy. As a detective story, it's also lacking, since we're already well aware of the core mystery before Holmes even arrives. It is clearly a propaganda piece from Doyle, but more interestingly there are echoes of the later pulp adventure tradition hidden in this story, including airships and German villains and convoluted conspiracies. If you replace "German" with "Nazi" or replace Holmes with a character like Doc Savage, it's striking how prescient this story is in tone and content.

The Case-Book of Sherlock Holmes

Preface

We arrive at *The Case-Book of Sherlock Holmes*. All these stories were written after World War I, which had a profound impact on Doyle (he lost a number of friends and family members in the war). Also, his growing interest in Spiritualism and séances made it harder for him to write in the Holmesean mindset. Further, he was just thoroughly tired of Holmes and still considered him to be beneath his more serious work. All this comes out in the preface to this book, written in 1927:

> *"And so, reader, farewell to Sherlock Holmes! I thank you for your past constancy, and can but hope that some return has been made in the shape of that distraction from the worries of life and stimulating change of thought which can only be found in the fairy kingdom of romance."*

That being said, there is also a lot of experimentation in this phase of his career (and I count "His Last Bow" as part of this phase, even though it was collected in the previous book). Within are multiple stories that explicitly stray from the formula, and the stories overall are darker and more menacing in tone. In many ways, they presage the coming American literary traditions of pulp and detective fiction. All in all, they are generally viewed as some of the weaker stories in the canon.

"The Adventure of the Mazarin Stone" (1921)

Doyle's lack of interest in Holmes and the Holmes formula is extremely clear in "The Mazarin Stone." The plot is an adaptation of "The Crown Diamond," a successful play that Doyle wrote that toured at the same time as this story was published. The fact that it was adapted from a play explains why the story all takes place in one room. The whole thing reads like a bad, exaggerated pastiche of Holmes, and not like Doyle's work at all.

Part of the reason for the feeling of pastiche is that there are a couple of elements that are clearly lifted from "The Empty House." A similar bust of Holmes was in that previous story, and both were made by Frenchmen — this one by "Tavernier, the French modeler," although the one in "The Empty House" was made by Monsieur Oscar Meunier of Grenoble. Also, there is another criminal across the street with an air-gun trained on 221B. Further, another anonymous inspector is mentioned — this time, Youghal of C.I.D. (although Holmes has always previously referred to that institution as "the Yard" instead of "C.I.D."). Billy the page is mentioned, but he's given a greatly exaggerated role and is implied to be much order than previous stories indicated. Finally, there is a lot more rough slang used in this story, which feels more like American detective fiction than Doyle's more high-class fare. Like "His Last Bow," this is the second story told from a third-person perspective, and also the second story in which Watson is not present for large parts of the action. (The story is written to seem as if Holmes may also not be present, but it is later revealed that he was, in fact, there.) There isn't even much of a mystery here — Holmes simply sets things up to trick two men into giving a confession.

How Holmes is portrayed is also markedly different. He is atypically sarcastic and witty in the story — certainly Holmes has been known for his sardonic wit, but here he comes across almost like a comedian, constantly unleashing his wit and pulling jokes on people. However, the story claims that Holmes seldom laughed, even though there are around 300 instances of Holmes laughing in the canon (and certainly that laughter is seen in certain portrayals of Holmes, most notably Jeremy Brett's). We do get a very Holmesian quote in the story ("I am a brain, Watson. The rest of me is a mere appendix."), and we see his obsession with technology in the use of the gramophone (which helps to date the case at least after 1900, and probably between 1902 and 1905), but this Holmes is very jarring and inconsistent with the one we know.

In all, this story feels like Doyle is just trying to cash in on his previous successes, although I might feel that way in part due to the tone of the preface.

The Problem of Thor Bridge (1922)

"The Problem of Thor Bridge" is probably most well-known for being the story with the first mention of Watson's infamous tin dispatch box:

Somewhere in the vaults of the bank of Cox and Co., at Charing Cross, there is a travel-worn and battered tin dispatch box with my name, John H. Watson, M. D., Late Indian Army, painted upon the lid. It is crammed with papers, nearly all of which are records of cases to illustrate the curious problems which Mr. Sherlock Holmes had at various times to examine.

True, Watson never actually served in the "Indian Army," which is a separate organization from the British Army that served in India (as Watson served in the Berkshires and the Northumberland Fusiliers), but it presents a fascinating list of non-canonical cases that have enflamed the imagination of pastiche writers for over a century. Also, since this is the second time Watson's middle initial is mentioned, I should mention that there has been some speculation about what the "H" stands for.

General consensus seems to circle around "Henry," but there's one other theory that I love: Dorothy L. Sayers proposes that it might actually stand for "Hamish," a Scotch equivalent for "James" (thus also neatly covering Mrs. Watson's slip of calling Watson "James" in "The Twisted Lip"). It appears I'm not the only one who likes this one, as "Hamish" is used for Watson in the BBC series *Sherlock*.

So with that introduction, we see that this is a refreshing return to form for Doyle after the miserable "Mazarin Stone," and it's one of the stronger stories in the book to boot. In fact, Doyle does some backtracking on his last two stories, having Watson claim that "I was either not present or played so small a part that [some stories] could only be told as by a third person." Holmes displays his particular brand of reverse snobbery with such lines as "Some of you rich men have to be taught that all the world cannot be bribed into condoning your offences." There's a great use of the classic device of the damning clue actually being the salvation of the accused (in this case, the revolver in the wardrobe), as well as the device of Holmes talking out his theories with Watson. There's also a fantastic bit of Holmes forgetting social niceties when on a case as he borrows Watson's revolver, ties it to a rock, lets them both fall into the water, and then asks someone else to get it back for him! There's even a little explanation of why Watson tends to carry a revolver on their cases:

"Watson," said he, "I have some recollection that you go armed upon these excursions of ours."

It was as well for him that I did so, for he took little care for his own safety when his mind was once absorbed by a problem so that more than once my revolver had been a good friend in need.

Some points of Victorian culture. There are a couple of examples of the unfortunate ethnic stereotyping common in the Victorian era: Americans are all "readier with pistols than our folk are," and South Americans all suffer from "a tropical nature." Suicide (or "self-murder" as it was legally known then) was not uncommon in London, but the proving of suicide caused different distributions in property, which is why it had to be investigated even if it couldn't be prosecuted (and why some suicides went through elaborate lengths to appear as if they were murders). There are references to the double-jury system of criminal prosecution between the police court and the coroner's court (although these days, a "coroner's jury" is called an inquest, and seems to have less legal weight). And finally, while I haven't been going into the minute studies of Sherlockian scholars too much in these essays, there's a great example of it inspired by this story: The reference to a "safety catch" on Watson's pistol helped Stanton O. Berg, a firearms consultant, to deduce that there is only one pistol that fits the timeframe of the story that has a safety catch — the Webley Mark III .380 caliber pocket revolver.

The Adventure of the Creeping Man (1923)

The best way to describe this story is to talk about a pastiche first. Bear with me for a bit.

In Nicholas Meyer's *The Seven-Per-Cent Solution*, Watson declares in his "Introductory" section that "I will speak not here of forgeries by other hands than mine, which include such drivel as 'The Lion's Mane,' 'The Mazarin Stone,' 'The Creeping Man,' and 'The Three Gables.'" The fact that other players in the Great Game have latched onto this as a potential explanation of

173

the quality of these stories is telling. "The Mazarin Stone" has already shown its own failings from top to bottom, so it's hard to refute Meyer's attempt to simply discount those four stories. (Although, to be fair, *The Seven-Per-Cent Solution* is probably one of the best Sherlock Holmes pastiches ever written, so it's hard to discount Meyer regardless. I highly recommend it, as well as his other two works, *The West End Horror* and *The Canary Trainer*.)

I cannot so easily dismiss this story as Meyer does, however. The flaws in "The Creeping Man" aren't as visible at the start, but the end puts the story firmly in the realm of science-fiction — it reads closer to Robert Louis Stevenson's *Dr. Jekyll and Mr. Hyde* or one of Doyle's own Professor Challenger stories than a Holmes story. However, this story is perhaps the seed that allowed for more fanciful Holmes pastiches involving the supernatural and the fantastic, and there have certainly been a number of anthologies on that topic in recent years (including *Gaslight Arcanum*, which I reviewed for FlamesRising.com). Like many of Doyle's later stories, that is a strong chance that this one is inspired by real events — in this case, Serge Voronoff, a Russian-French surgeon who grafted ape testicle tissue into humans under the hypothesis that it rejuvenated the patient. As such, I have to take the stance that Doyle may have considered this story to be scientific instead of "romantic," and that the "science" presented here is as flawed as phrenology, but still considered to be accurate in the minds of the characters. The amount of discussion attempting to reconcile the facts in the story is immense.

For all of Meyer's wishing it were otherwise, the story *is* canonical, and from a canonical stance, there are plenty of trivial details to make it worthwhile. For one, it ties itself well to other stories, between the mention of the tin box from "Thor Bridge" and expounding on a point presented in "The Copper Beeches." Holmes also repeats a quote from "Thor Bridge": "We can but try." We learn that this is one of Holmes' last cases in 1903, and some unkind Sherlockians have intimated that his complete failure in this case may have been the reason for said retirement. Watson is not only no longer living at Baker Street, but he also has a practice again, which makes for a new time-frame for consideration (post-Hiatus-post-Baker-Street). We get our first mention of Holmes' post-Watson organization which will come up again in upcoming stories: The mysterious "Mercer" mentioned in this story, as well as Shinwell (mentioned in "The Illustrious Client") and Langdale Pike (in "The Three Gables"). It also contains my favorite telegram from Holmes to Watson: "Come at once if convenient — if inconvenient come all the same. S. H." (which was reused to perfect effect by Steven Moffat as text messages in the episode "A Study in Pink" in *Sherlock*).

One of the more interesting canonical bits, though, comes when Watson talks about how he had become an institution in the later part of their friendship — specifically, Watson's role not only as an ally when a case is active, but also as a foil, someone with which to sound out ideas. At first, this seems like an explanation of the implicit relationship between Holmes and Watson, but it's more subtle than that — Holmes naturally has to explain his mindset as a narrative device, and this allows for a bit of character development simultaneously, turning a narrative necessity into an expansion of the dynamic. More fascinating to me, however, is that I read this story after being told by a programmer friend at work about "rubber duck debugging," a method in which a programmer explains his code line-by-line to a small rubber duck sitting at his desk, which helped him to find flaws in his reasoning. This idea of "thinking out loud" isn't new, but it's still just as useful today as it was in the early 20th century. As such, it ends up working on *three* levels: narrative device, exploration of characterization, and reference to an actual method of problem-solving.

For all this, the ending completely ruins what could have been a solid Holmes story. Even attempting to frame it as "Victorian science" makes it hard to take this story seriously. Which is a shame, because it could have been so much better if only science really worked that way.

The Adventure of the Sussex Vampire (1924)

The biggest thing this story brings to the canon is one of the most evocative apocryphal case references:

> *"Matilda Briggs was not the name of a young woman, Watson," said Holmes in a reminiscent voice. "It was a ship which is associated with the giant rat of Sumatra, a story for which the world is not yet prepared."*

This casual reference by Holmes has probably spawned more pastiches than any other. *The Spider Woman* and *In Pursuit of Algiers* (both Basil Rathbone and Nigel Bruce movies) contain references to it, and novels such as *The Holmes-Dracula File* by Fred Saberhagen, *The Giant Rat of Sumatra* by Rick Boyer, and *Sherlock Holmes and the Giant Rat of Sumatra* by Alan Vanneman address the case directly, just to name a few. The idea has even extended outside of Holmes to properties such as the Hardy Boys and Doctor Who!

And speaking of Dracula, the reference to vampires in this story have led to a couple of pastiches involving the most famous vampire in literature, including the previously-mentioned Saberhagen novel, as well as *Sherlock Holmes vs. Dracula: The Adventure of the Sanguinary Count* written by Loren D. Estleman. I could probably write a whole essay just on the Victorian fascination with vampires even before *Dracula* was published, but suffice it to say that the concept was as known to Victorian culture as it is to us now, and it isn't as strange of a match-up as it might appear at first.

Next to *Hound*, this is the most popular story of Holmes investigating a situation that appears supernatural but turns out to be perfectly mundane. However, right after "The Creeping Man," it seems a bit arbitrary: scientists becoming monkeys due to an injection is plausible, but vampires aren't? Regardless of the context, though, one of the most iconic quotes of Holmes' attitude towards the supernatural is in this story:

"This agency stands flat-footed upon the ground, and there it must remain. The world is big enough for us. No ghosts need apply."

As usual with the better stories in the canon, there are lots of good bits about Holmes and Watson here. There's a nice nod to "The Gloria Scott" here. In "The Creeping Man," Holmes mentioned how the study of dogs can give an indication of the household that owns it, and here we see a perfect example of that idea in practice. We learn that while Holmes is meticulous in collecting information, he rarely gives credit to the source he got it from. Watson played rugby for Blackheath, which was an amateur rugby club formed in 1858. Holmes admits that while he prefers to not form theories without data, he is still prone to it sometimes.

Finally, a reference to "the dry chuckle which was his nearest approach to a laugh" shows how inconsistently Holmes' laughter is portrayed in the canon (cross-reference this with his laughter in "The Mazarin Stone").

Again, in such an uneven volume, this stands out as a pure and classic Holmes tale. Holmes' stance on the supernatural is consistent with that in *The Hound of the Baskervilles*. It's surprising that this is such a pragmatic case, as Doyle was quite firmly in the grip of Spiritualism at this point, but it's good despite (or perhaps because of) Doyle's beliefs.

The Adventure of the Three Garridebs (1924)

This isn't one of the worst stories in the collection, but it isn't very original. The plot is very similar to "The Red-Headed League" and "The Stock-Broker's Clerk" (taking an unusual aspect of an innocent man and using it to find an elaborate method to get them out of the way). It has a couple of interesting points, such as being the first use of a telephone and telephone directory in the canon and the interesting emphasis that Holmes places on the danger of counterfeiting ("... the counterfeiter stands in a class by himself as a public danger.") There's also the infamous and fleeting reference to Holmes refusing a knighthood, although he accepted a Legion of Honor from the French President in "The Golden Pince-Nez." This seems less concerned with Holmes' own personality as it is Conan Doyle's, who felt positively forced into accepting a knighthood from Edward VII at around the same time.

There is one scene that makes this story worth reading, when Watson is shot during the course of the story. Holmes' reaction is wonderful, and consistent with "The Devil's Foot":

"You're not hurt, Watson? For God's sake, say that you are not hurt!"

It was worth a wound — it was worth many wounds — to know the depth of loyalty and love which lay behind that cold mask. The clear, hard eyes were dimmed for a moment, and the firm lips were shaking. For the one and only time I caught a glimpse of a great heart as well as of a great brain. All my years of humble but single-minded service culminated in that moment of revelation.

Of course, that isn't the "one and only time," but it is a great sentiment nonetheless.

The Adventure of the Illustrious Client (1924)

On the heels of the largely-forgettable "The Three Garribs" comes one of the better stories of the collection (and one of Doyle's personal favorites). This is actually a great story for information about the changes in the relationship between Holmes and Watson in the 20th century. Specifically, they are older, and this is probably the reason why they both like Turkish baths (which was also mentioned in "Lady Frances Carfax"). This is another case that is post-Hiatus-post-Baker-Street: Watson is again no longer with Holmes, having his own rooms on Queen Anne Street. Watson is also still a doctor at this stage, as at one point he mentions having "pressing professional business." Holmes mentions his new assistant, Shinwell Johnson, who has started working with him at the turn of the century (which implies that Watson moved out of Baker Street at some point before the turn of the century). We learn that Watson is nearly as well-known at the Yard as Holmes. Watson even admits to editing Holmes:

"Then he told the story, which I would repeat in this way. His hard, dry statement needs some little editing to soften it into the terms of real life."

There are some interesting parallels to past stories, however — not a complete retread like the previous case, but nice notes and elements seen again. There are mentions of Moriarty and Moran, and we learn that Moran is still alive at this point (and presumably still in jail). Holmes' expertise with the stick keeps him in good stead again. Like "The Six Napoleons," Holmes manipulates the press for his own ends. There is yet another woman in the canon named "Violet" — this time, Violet de Merville. There's a reference to Simpson's (more specifically, Simpson's-In-The-Strand) — a popular London restaurant referenced not only a few times in the canon, but by other writers, such as E. M. Forster and P. G. Wodehouse. And Holmes' sexism comes forth.

"Woman's heart and mind are insoluble puzzles to the male. Murder might be condoned or explained, and yet some smaller offence might rankle."

However, his perspective on women is more complex than it was previously:

"Women of the De Merville type do not act like that. She would love him the more as a disfigured martyr."

The exchange between the Baron and Holmes is particularly interesting to note. It is similar in civility as the one between Moriarty and Holmes in "The Final Problem" (the gentleman criminal and the gentleman detective is in full display here), but it doesn't quite have the depths of mental chess that

Moriarty's exchange had. This might be due to the place in our collective culture that Moriarty has, but I feel that the Baron is an adequate foil for Holmes, even if he is not the most notorious. It's also a bit unusual that the Baron claims that his personality has caused a post-hypnotic influence. Granted, it's indicative of the 1920s fascination with hypnotism, but otherwise it's an odd note.

On a side note, there are a couple of other cultural references, such as "nark" being a term for informing to the police even this far back in time. Attack by acid wasn't uncommon — it was a crime officially called "vitriol-throwing" (which also happened in "The Blue Carbuncle"). The reference to card-playing as an analogy for bluffing is also a nice insight into the Victorian mind: "Not a color card there, Mr. Holmes, nothing but the smallest of the small." (A "color card" is what we'd call a face card now: a jack, queen, king, and sometimes an ace.)

The most intriguing part of the story for me, though, is the continuation of the conflict between Holmes and Watson in regards to Watson's ability to lie. In "The Dying Detective," Holmes held back his true medical condition, because he felt Watson wouldn't be able to convince people otherwise. This time, Holmes is asking Watson to exaggerate the nature of his injuries. Has Watson become a better liar in the intervening years? However, as Watson points out:

"There was a curious secretive streak in the man which led to many dramatic effects, but left even his closest friend guessing as to what his exact plans might be. He pushed to an extreme the axiom that the only safe plotter was he who plotted alone. I was nearer him than anyone else, and yet I was always conscious of the gap between."

Watson crams on knowledge of Chinese pottery in order to carry out a task for Holmes. This is not the inquisitive, confused Watson of the early canon — he simply does as he is asked. But sadly, Holmes' observation of Watson's ability to lie turns out to be accurate — he bumbles the conversation with the Baron.

Finally, there is the speculation on the identity of the titular "illustrious client." There are a number of theories about this, but it's generally assumed to be King Edward — the same person implied as the client in "The Beryl Coronet" when he was the Prince of Wales.

The Adventure of the Three Gables (1926)

Ah, racism. After such unusually tolerant stories about race such as "The Yellow Face," we get Steve Dixie. He's a negro and a thug that calls Holmes "Massar" and is described as a "savage." Further, Holmes insults Steve's smell and commends Watson for not breaking "his wooly head." Some have attempted to excuse this as more relevant to Dixie's standing as a criminal and boxer than his race, as it's possible that the reference to smell is actually related to class. Some parts of London, such as the Jago, were not only so notoriously dangerous that policemen travelled in pairs, but their squalor was also legendary, which may account for Dixie's smell. Some scholars have even tried to excuse Doyle by blaming Holmes, claiming that his treatment of Dixie is consistent with the erratic behavior known to lengthy cocaine abusers (in particular, this theory is mentioned in "Subcutaneously, My Dear Watson: Sherlock Holmes and the Cocaine Habit" by Jack Tracy and Jim Berkey.) On the other hand, this story was written three decades after "The Yellow Face," and we know that Doyle had very different beliefs later in life than he held when he was a younger man, so it could very well be exactly what it appears to be. But whether Doyle was being racist or classist (and I am still inclined to the former), Doyle's writing is far less tolerant than it was previously — the sheer volume of epitaphs against Dixie in such a short space are hard to ignore.

Then we turn to the other stereotype — the exotic and evil woman, Mrs. Isadora Klein: "So roguish and exquisite did she look as she stood before us with a challenging smile that I felt of all Holmes' criminals this was the one whom he would find it hardest to face." Thankfully, Holmes is immune to the charms of the fairer sex, a fact which some fanfic writers have eagerly leapt upon. She is very much the *femme fatale* (or, as Holmes says, the *belle dame sans merci* — the beautiful woman without compassion). And much like the role of the *femme fatale*, she uses her charms to coax the detective into committing a crime on her behalf — in this case, leading Holmes to take justice into his hands and "compound a felony as usual." While we have seen Holmes do this several times in the canon, this time it feels wrong — Holmes is clearly taking money to cover up a crime, even if he is just passing the money on to his client.

There are other elements that make this feel more like a bad pastiche than Doyle's work. There is the usual Scotland Yard detective, and yet he is never given a name. Holmes makes a number of mistakes in the story: Why does Holmes tell his client to have her lawyer stay with her, and why does she ignore this advice? He later admits that he should have had Watson stay — why didn't he? And for all the stories in which Holmes is shown to be absorbed by the problems of these crimes, here he says "Surely no man would take up my profession if it were not that danger attracts him," which sounds much more like Watson's motivation than Holmes'.

No, even the introduction of the tantalizing Langdale Pike into Holmes' organization, the "human book of reference upon all matters of social scandal," does little to salvage this weak story. It feels like a hardboiled American detective story forcefully injected into a Holmes mold, and this time Doyle does a terrible Raymond Chandler impression.

The Adventure of the Blanched Soldier (1926)

"The Blanched Soldier" is one of two stories written from the perspective of Holmes. As a result, it contains a number of surprising insights into Holmes' innermost thoughts, particularly how he sees Watson (who, by this point in January 1903, has married again).

For example, in the first sentence, Holmes takes a swing at Watson: "The ideas of my friend Watson, though limited, are exceedingly pertinacious." Later, he comes to admit he may have been wrong in some of his previous criticisms of Watson:

Perhaps I have rather invited this persecution, since I have often had occasion to point out to him how superficial are his own accounts and to accuse him of pandering to popular taste instead of confining himself rigidly to facts and figures. "Try it yourself, Holmes!" he has retorted, and I am compelled to admit that, having taken my pen in my hand, I do begin to realize that the matter must be presented in such a way as may interest the reader.

Later Holmes continues to speak highly (and yet backhandedly) about Watson:

Speaking of my old friend and biographer, I would take this opportunity to remark that if I burden myself with a companion in my various little inquiries it is not done out of sentiment or caprice, but it is that Watson has some remarkable characteristics of his own to which in his modesty he has given small attention amid his exaggerated estimates of my own performances. A confederate who foresees your conclusions and course of action is always dangerous, but one to whom each development comes as a perpetual surprise, and to whom the future is always a closed book, is indeed an ideal helpmate.

Near the end, Holmes has a surprisingly tender moment: "And here it is that I miss my Watson. By cunning questions and ejaculations of wonder he could elevate my simple art, which is but systematized common sense, into a prodigy."

We also learn why Holmes regularly blurts out deductions about his clients ("I have found it wise to impress clients with a sense of power...."), and his tendency to assume the people around him are smarter than they really are shows up in this narrative ("It presented, as the astute reader will have already perceived, few difficulties in its solution"). There's an interesting (if garbled) reference to "The Priory School," and Holmes laments his inability to be dramatic when he is writing the story himself:

I passed on into the study with my case complete. Alas, that I should have to show my hand so when I tell my own story! It was by concealing such links in the chain that Watson was enabled to produce his meretricious finales.

I ended up quoting more than writing on this story, but really the insights we get about Holmes in his own words are the only noteworthy parts of "The Blanched Soldier." The story itself isn't amazing (it's a bit long on the monologues), but it's solid enough to showcase the Master Detective's inner process in this new format.

The Adventure of the Lion's Mane (1926)

"The Lion's Mane," right after "The Blanched Soldier," is the second (and final) story narrated by Holmes. This story is also noteworthy because it is the only one set after Holmes' retirement, and thus doesn't involve Watson in any way. The loss of Watson is again keenly felt by Holmes:

At this period of my life the good Watson had passed almost beyond my ken. An occasional week-end visit was the most that I ever saw of him. Thus I must act as my own chronicler. Ah! had he but been with me, how much he might have made of so wonderful a happening and of my eventual triumph against every difficulty!

In retired life, Holmes references "his old housekeeper," although never by name. In "His Last Bow" we learn her name is Martha, and there's nothing here to contradict that fact. Further, Mrs. Hudson is never given a first name, and thus many fans consider Holmes' housekeeper to be Martha Hudson. At first it seems a bit of a stretch that Holmes would suddenly stop calling a woman by her last name and use her first one instead, but as mentioned it was the Victorian fashion to refer to people by their last names whenever possible, using first names only for family (such as in the case of Mycroft). Around the Edwardian era, though, it became more accepted for friends and close acquaintances to use first names instead. It is telling, however, that Holmes continues to refer to his friend as "Watson" — possibly out of habit.

But it is the post-retirement Holmes' quirks that fascinate me the most. In his late life, he likes to swim and keep bees. Holmes' methods of deduction have evolved a little (including a mention of photographing evidence, something not previously detailed). It's not surprising that Holmes remains "an omnivorous reader with a strangely retentive memory for trifles." What is surprising, though, is how Holmes reacts to the beauty of a woman:

Women have seldom been an attraction to me, for my brain has always governed my heart, but I could not look upon her perfect clear-cut face, with all the soft freshness of the downlands in her delicate coloring, without realizing that no young man would cross her path unscathed.... Maud Bellamy will always remain in my memory as a most complete and remarkable woman.

Later he even mentions that "I value a woman's instinct in such matters." What a change from the man who was inherently distrustful of women!

In fact, as you dig into the story, a number of details about post-retirement Holmes feel a bit odd. The Great Detective seems particularly stumped by this case (although likely this is because there would be little other way to provide suspense from Doyle's perspective), and at one point he confesses to being at "the limit of my powers." More specifically, Holmes admits to being "culpably slow" about whether the victim had been swimming or not, when a simple examination of the body to determine if it was wet would have sufficed. Further, a Holmes that has retired to avoid all mental stimulation seems a very long way from the man who needed cocaine just to get through days of boredom. He also muses on the "beautiful, faithful nature of dogs," which is a different stance from the man who experimented on dogs in his youth. Finally, Holmes' description of his own mental processes seems a very long way from his "brain attic" at the start of the canon!

> *You will know, or Watson has written in vain, that I hold a vast store of out-of-the-way knowledge without scientific system, but very available for the needs of my work. My mind is like a crowded box-room with packets of all sorts stowed away therein — so many that I may well have but a vague perception of what was there.*

Much of this can be chalked up to age — we are very rarely the same people in our late years that we were in our youth. It's not hard to believe that Holmes has merely changed over time, and has convinced himself that he was always this way rather than accept the contradictions in his nature. This is the stance I tend to hold to, because it not only connects with my views on human nature, but it also reinforces the complexity of Holmes' nature as a man. Of course, other scholars have proposed different theories to explain the inconsistencies. One of my favorites is from Mary Ann Kluge, who simply believes that the case was actually solved by Watson!

There are two other minor points of interest. Historically, the reference in the story to J. G. Wood and his book are factual, and he really was nearly killed by Cyanea Capillata. As a writer, I appreciate that in the original manuscript for "The Lion's Mane," there were several references to a "Dr. Mordhouse," a naturalist also in the area. He was excised from the story in a later draft, and many of his actions and lines were given to Stackhurst and Holmes. Doyle, like many good writers, understood the value of cutting extraneous characters to make a story tighter.

The Adventure of the Retired Colourman (1926)

After two stories told from Holmes' perspective, we're back to a first-person story told by Watson. The classic formula is fully on display in this story, and there are some great moments between the two friends. For example, Watson is sent off as an "understudy" to collect evidence (an act that is retold later for good effect — it not only helps pacing, but also allows Holmes to comments on Watson's efforts). Watson starts to explain what he's found:

"... Right in the middle of them, a little island of ancient culture and comfort, lies this old home, surrounded by a high sun-baked wall mottled with lichens and topped with moss, the sort of wall —"

"Cut out the poetry, Watson," said Holmes severely. "I note that it was a high brick wall."

Holmes again chides Watson for missing details (like he did in "The Solitary Cyclist"), but at least this time he is more moderate, and often praises Watson's observations, if not his deductions: "No one else would have done better. Some possibly not so well. But clearly you have missed some vital points."

We see Holmes lamenting his relationship with the Yard (and how they send "incurables" to him), his preferences for city life (and "the horrors of a country inn" — quite at odds with his eventual retirement), and the fact that he considered burglary as an alternative profession. He remarks on Watson's abilities to sway women, and the fact that there's a telephone in Baker Street (previously mentioned in "The Illustrious Client" and "The Three Garridebs"). We also learn of a supposed rival to Holmes — Barker in Surrey — that we haven't heard of before (or since).

Many scholars have tried to link him to other characters in the canon, most notably the detective in "colored glasses" noticed by Watson in "The Empty House."

Historically, there's a reference to Watson's old school number. In boarding schools, each pupil was given an identification number, which is kept throughout the student's career at that school. There's also a passing mention of "Broadmoor," which was a prison specifically for criminal lunatics (and is now a psychiatric hospital).

One thing that irritates me is that I've seen multiple references in my research that the story is set in 1898, but I can't find anything in my version of the text that explicitly says that. Baring-Gould seems to confirm it, though, so I'm not inclined to argue the point. However, this again brings up one of the irritations of Holmes scholarship. There are three different "official" versions of the text: the version published in the *Strand* magazine, the version eventually compiled into the British publications, and the version that was edited for the American publications. For casual reading the differences are largely negligible, but as you dive more and more into the study of Holmes and try to reconcile or even just track facts, time and again you'll run into some flavor of "oh, that was mentioned in some other version of the text." Some days, I feel like studying the different translations of the Bible would be easier.

The Adventure of the Veiled Lodger (1927)

This is the shortest of the stories, so there's not a lot to say. It's not a mystery at all. Not in the "it was a pretty simple problem" sense, but in the "Holmes and Watson do nothing but listen to other people" sense. Holmes does nothing, because there is nothing to do.

Granted, there are some cool bits. I love the return to vague references that imply a world outside the stories, as when Watson talks about the attempts to destroy his papers. I enjoy Holmes' blatant sarcasm as he says "Mrs. Merrilow does not object to tobacco, Watson, if you wish to indulge your filthy habits."

As I make my way through the canon, I've largely abandoned any sane attempt to date the stories, but there's a problem in this story that I just can't let slip past. In the story, Watson claims that Holmes was in active practice for 23 years, and that Watson was taking notes for only 17 of them. Holmes' part of this is simple: Assuming you don't count the three years of the Great Hiatus as being "active practice," and you add 26 to the retirement year of 1903, you get 1877. This coincides with "The Musgrave Ritual," which many chronologists set at 1879. However, Watson joined Holmes in 1881 or 1882, which only accounts for four or five years.

There are a lot of theories to account for the missing year or two (the most plausible of which being that Watson didn't actually take notes of the cases for a while, although this does contract *A Study in Scarlet*), but at the end of the day I have to accept that it's just an error and be irritated by it. Which is fine, because the whole story irritates me. It's not terrible, but it certainly isn't good.

The Adventure of Shoscombe Old Place (1927)

We find another Yard detective — this time, Merivale. Merivale is the only policeman Holmes calls friend, and only one of three men that he considered a friend in the entire canon (the others are Charlie Peace and, of course, Watson). Holmes uses more card-playing references, but seems to have forgotten all that he knew about horse-racing from "Silver Blaze," enough though this story is dates after that one (roughly around 1902). We finally get confirmation of Watson's gambling habit, which previously had only been eluded to:

> *"By the way, Watson, you know something of racing?"*
>
> *"I ought to. I pay for it with about half my wound pension."*

We see Holmes observing dogs, praising microscopes, and waxing poetic about fishing, and we get another reference to "Queer Street" (the previous one was in "The Second Stain"). He does not, however, take the law into his own hands, and seems positively against the idea, claiming:

> *"[It] was my duty to bring the facts to light, and there I must leave it. As to the morality or decency of your conduct, it is not for me to express an opinion."*

You've certainly "expressed an opinion" on such things before, Holmes!

Perhaps even more unusual, Watson becomes surprisingly snobbish. His reluctance to accept Sir Robert as a murderer is at odds with not only his previous comments about Sir Robert nearly murdering someone, but also at odds with the line of upper class villains he'd encountered previously (including Moriarty!).

There are a couple of references to "Jews" in this story, but it's really Victorian slang for "moneylender." And thus we end this tour of the canonical Sherlock Holmes: on an awkward note of casual racism.

The Best Stories

Sixty stories. Nine books. That's a lot of reading to get through, and it's a very small portion of the ink spilled over Sherlock Holmes outside of Doyle. So, which ones are the best?

Doyle himself selected that he thought were the best of his short stories in an essay for *Strand Magazine*. He picked twelve stories and ordered them from most to least favorite. In a later revision of the list, he added seven more, for a total of nineteen:

1. "The Speckled Band"
2. "The Red-Headed League"
3. "The Dancing Men"
4. "The Final Problem"
5. "A Scandal in Bohemia"
6. "The Empty House"
7. "The Five Orange Pips"
8. "The Second Stain"
9. "The Devil's Foot"
10. "The Priory School"
11. "The Musgrave Ritual"
12. "The Reigate Squires"
13. "Silver Blaze"
14. "The Bruce-Partington Plans"
15. "The Crooked Man"
16. "The Man with the Twisted Lip"
17. "The Greek Interpreter"
18. "The Resident Patient"
19. "The Naval Treaty"

As for me, I disagree with some Doyle's choices. I have my own list of favorites.

Of the novels, the best is far and away *The Hound of the Baskervilles*. There's a reason why it's the book most people know of when they think of Holmes, and why the deerstalker hat is so well known (even if it only shows up in this book and one or two other places).

Of the short stories, I've narrowed it down to my top ten (and let me tell you, that was an agonizing process):

1. "A Scandal in Bohemia": Although the first two novels predate this story, I feel this is where Doyle really finds his feet with Holmes.
2. "The Final Problem"/"The Empty House": Yes, I'm cheating here, but I really feel these are both one connected story, and they also comprise most of the canonical references to Moriarty. Absolutely gripping.
3. "The Blue Carbuncle": The first place where I deviate from Doyle, but for purely personal reasons. This story is such a part of my childhood that I can't possibly be rational about it.
4. "The Red-Headed League": Doyle uses this plot a few times throughout the canon, but the first time is, to me, the best.
5. "The Musgrave Ritual": The actual ritual is used in various Sherlockian societies, and it's very likely the seed for the cliché of "the butler did it."
6. "Charles Augustus Milverton": The other place where I disagree with Doyle. Milverton is probably the second-best villain in the canon (and, at the time of this

writing, is announced as the replacement villain in BBC's *Sherlock*, so clearly other people think so as well!).

7. "The Second Stain": Probably the best example of the Lestrade/Holmes dynamic.

8. "The Bruce-Partington Plans": Big use of Mycroft, a great spy story, and a good companion to "The Second Stain."

9. "The Devil's Foot": The story isn't as good as it could be, but the powerful exploration of the friendship between Holmes and Watson is just amazing.

10. "Silver Blaze": I had a tough time between this and "The Five Orange Pips," but the tracking scene and some of the dialogue just manages to put this into the top ten for me.

Chronology of the cases

Time and again I have mentioned the problems and difficulties in trying to date the cases in a chronological order. I have personally given up trying to reconcile the chronology, but that has not stopped others from attempting it. To offer some insight into this problem, I present two of the more widely accepted chronologies: William S. Baring-Gould's (from *The Annotated Sherlock Holmes*) and Leslie Klinger's (from *The New Annotated Sherlock Holmes*). I also have one from Mike Ashley from *The New Sherlock Holmes Adventures*, an anthology of short story pastiches. Since I'm partial to Klinger's timeline, I present that one as the primary timeline, and note the opinions of Baring-Gould (WBG) and Mike Ashley (MA) with each story.

Early Holmes

"The Gloria Scott" — 1874 (WBG Sun, Jul 12 to Tues, Aug 4, & Tues, Sept 22, 1874; MA 1873/4)

"The Musgrave Ritual" — 1879 (WBG Thur, Oct 2, 1879; MA 1878)

Pre-Mary Morstan

A Study in Scarlet — 1881 (WBG Fri, Mar 4, to Mon, Mar 7, 1881; MA March 1881)

"The Speckled Band" — 1883 (WBG Fri, Apr 6, 1883; MA April 1883)

"The Beryl Coronet" — 1886 (WBG Fri, Dec 19 to Sat, Dec 20, 1890; MA February 1882)

"The Resident Patient" — 1887 (WBG Wed, Oct 6 to Thur, Oct 7, 1886; MA October 1881)

"The Reigate Squires" — 1887 (WBG Thur, Apr 14 to Tues Apr 26, 1887; MA April 1887)

The Valley of Fear — 1888 (WBG Sat, Jan 7 to Sun, Jan 8, 1888; MA January 1888)

"The Noble Bachelor" — 1888 (WBG Fri, Oct 8, 1886; MA September 1888)

"The Yellow Face" — 1888 (WBG Sat, Apr 7, 1888; MA April 1886)

"The Greek Interpreter" — 1888 (WBG Wed, Sept 12, 1888; MA July/August 1888)

The Sign of Four — 1888 (WBG Tues, Sept 18 to Fri, Sept 21, 1888; MA September 1888)

Post-Mary Morstan

"Silver Blaze" — 1888 (WBG Thur, Sept 25 and Tues, Sept 30, 1890; MA October 1887)

"The Cardboard Box" — 1888 (WBG Sat, Aug 31 to Mon, Sept 2, 1889; MA August 1888)

"A Scandal in Bohemia" — 1889 (WBG Fri, May 20 to Sun, May 22, 1887; MA March 1889)

"The Man with the Twisted Lip" — 1889 (WBG Sat, Jun 18 to Sun, Jun 19, 1887; MA June 1889)

"A Case of Identity" — 1889 (WBG Tues, Oct 18 to Wed, Oct 19, 1887; MA May/June 1889)

"The Blue Carbuncle" — 1889 (WBG Tues, Dec 27, 1887; MA December 1889)

"The Five Orange Pips" — 1889 (WBG Thur, Sept 29 to Fri, Sept 30, 1887; MA September 1889)

"The Boscombe Valley Mystery" — 1889 (WBG Sat, Jun 8 to Sun, Jun 9, 1889; MA June 1890)

"The Stock-Broker's Clerk" — 1889 (WBG Sat, Jun 15, 1889; MA June 1889)

"The Naval Treaty" — 1889 (WBG Tues, Jul 30 to Thur, Aug 1, 1889; MA July 1889)

"The Engineer's Thumb" — 1889 (WBG Sat, Sept 7 to Sun, Sept 8, 1889; MA June 1889)

The Hound of the Baskervilles — 1889 (WBG Tues, Sept 25 to Sat, Oct 20, 1888; MA October 1888)

"The Crooked Man" — 1889 (WBG Wed, Sept 11 to Thur, Sept 12, 1889; MA August 1889)

"The Red-Headed League" — 1890 (WBG Sat, Oct 29 to Sun, Oct 30, 1887; MA October 1890)

"The Copper Beeches" — 1890 (WBG Fri, Apr 5 to Sat, Apr 20, 1889; MA April/May 1885)

"The Dying Detective" — 1890 (WBG Sat, Nov 19, 1887; MA November 1890)

"The Final Problem" — 1891 (WBG Fri, Apr 24 to Mon, May 4, 1891; MA April/May 1891)

Post-Hiatus

"The Empty House" — 1894 (WBG Thurs, Apr 5, 1894; MA February 1894)

"The Second Stain" — 1894 (WBG Tues, Oct 12, to Fri, Oct 15, 1886; MA March 1894)

"The Golden Pince-Nez" — 1894 (WBG Wed, Nov 14 to Thur, Nov 15, 1894; MA November 1894)

"The Norwood Builder" — 1894 (WBG Tues, Aug 20 to Wed. Aug 21, 1895; MA August 1894)

"Wisteria Lodge" — 1895 (WBG Mon, Mar 24 to Sat, Mar 29, 1890; MA March 1894)

"The Three Students" — 1895 (WBG Fri, Apr 5 to Sat, Apr 6, 1895; MA March 1895)

"The Solitary Cyclist" — 1895 (WBG Sat, Apr 13 to Sat, Apr 20, 1895; MA April 1895)

"Black Peter" — 1895 (WBG Wed, Jul 3 to Fri, Jul 5, 1895; MA July 1895)

"The Bruce-Partington Plans" — 1895 (WBG Thur, Nov 21 to Sat, Nov 23, 1895; MA November 1895)

"The Veiled Lodger" — 1896 (WBG Oct 1896; MA October 1896)

"The Sussex Vampire" — 1896 (WBG Thurs, Nov 19 to Sat, Nov 21, 1896; MA November 1896)

"The Missing Three-Quarter" — 1896 (WBG Tues, Dec 8 to Thurs, Dec 10, 1896; MA December 1897)

"The Abbey Grange" — 1897 (WBG Sat, Jan 23, 1897; MA January 1897)

"The Devil's Foot" — 1897 (WBG Tues, Mar 16 to Sat, Mar 20, 1897; MA March 1897)

"The Dancing Men" — 1898 (WBG Wed, Jul 27 to Wed, Aug 10 and Sat, Aug 13, 1898; MA July 1897)

"The Retired Colourman" — 1899 (WBG Thur, Jul 28 to Sat, Jul 30, 1898; MA July/August 1898)

"Charles Augustus Milverton" — 1899 (WBG Thur, Jan 5 to Sat, Jan 14, 1899; MA January 1887)

"The Six Napoleons" — 1900 (WBG Fri, Jun 8 to Sun, Jun 10, 1900; MA May 1900)

"The Priory School" — 1901 (WBG Thur, May 16 to Sat, May 18, 1901; MA May 1901)

"Disappearance of Lady Frances Carfax" — 1901 (WBG Tues, Jul 1 to Fri, Jul 18, 1902; MA Summer 1896)

"Thor Bridge" — 1901 (WBG Thur, Oct 4 to Fri, Oct 5, 1900; MA October 1901)

"Shoscombe Old Place" — 1902 (WBG Tues, May 6 to Wed, May 7, 1902; MA May 1902)

"The Three Garridebs" — 1902 (WBG Thur, Jun 26 to Fri, Jun 27, 1902; MA June 1902)

"The Three Gables" — 1902 (WBG Tues, May 26 to Wed, May 27, 1903; MA June 1903)

"The Illustrious Client" — 1902 (WBG Wed, Sept 3 to Tues, Sept 16, 1902; MA September 1902)

"The Red Circle" — 1902 (WBG Wed, Sept 24 to Thurs, Sept 25, 1902; MA February 1897)

Post-Baker Street

"The Blanched Soldier" — 1903 (WBG Wed, Jan 7 to Mon, Jan 12, 1903; MA January 1903)

"The Mazarin Stone" — 1903 (WBG Summer 1903; MA June 1903)

"The Creeping Man" — 1903 (WBG Sun, Sept 6 to Mon, Sept 14; Tues, Sept 22, 1903; MA September 1903)

Post-Retirement

"The Lion's Mane" — 1907 (WBG Tues, Jul 27 to Thur, Aug 3, 1909; MA July 1907)

"His Last Bow" — 1914 (WBG Sun, Aug 2, 1914; MA August 1914)

Also from MX Publishing

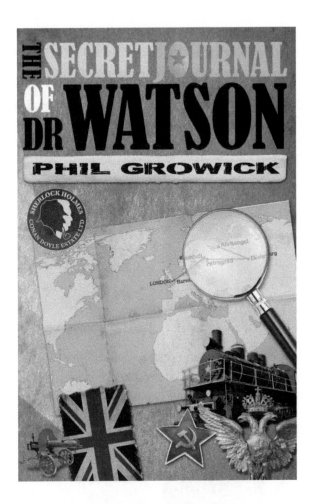

The Secret Journal of Dr Watson

www.mxpublishing.com

Also from MX Publishing

Winners of the 2011 Howlett Literary Award (Sherlock Holmes book of the year) for '**The Norwood Author**'

From the world's largest Sherlock Holmes publishers dozens of new novels from the top Holmes authors.

www.mxpublishing.com

Including our bestselling short story collections 'Lost Stories of Sherlock Holmes' , 'The Outstanding Mysteries of Sherlock Holmes', 'Untold Adventures of Sherlock Holmes' (and the sequel 'Studies in Legacy) and 'Sherlock Holmes in Pursuit'.

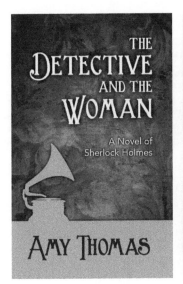 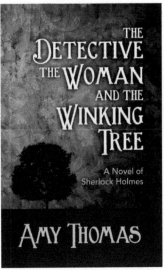

Two acclaimed novels featuring 'The Woman', Irene Adler
teaming up with Sherlock Holmes

Links

The Publishers are proud to support the Save Undershaw campaign — the campaign to save and restore Sir Arthur Conan Doyle's former home. Undershaw is where he brought Sherlock Holmes back to life, and should be preserved for future generations of Holmes fans.

Save Undershaw   www.saveundershaw.com

Sherlockology   www.sherlockology.com

MX Publishing   www.mxpublishing.com

You can read more about Sir Arthur Conan Doyle and Undershaw in Alistair Duncan's book (share of royalties to the Undershaw Preservation Trust) — An Entirely New Country and in the amazing compilation Sherlock's Home — The Empty House (all royalties to the Trust).

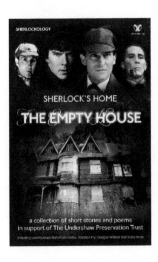

Lightning Source UK Ltd.
Milton Keynes UK
UKHW020654190722
406066UK00009B/998